BANDIGOAT

A COLLECTION OF STRANGE & HORRIBLE TALES

BLAFT

Chennai

Published in India in 2025 by
Blaft Publications Pvt. Ltd.

Paperback ISBN 978-93-80636-78-8
Hardcover ISBN 978-93-80636-79-5

Cover illustration / Bandigoat mispronunciation by Misha Michael a.k.a. Madame Bandigoat

Cover design by Radha Sunder

Blaft Publications Pvt. Ltd.
4/192 Ellaiamman Koil St.
Neelankarai
Chennai 600115
https://blaft.com

Printed at Sudarsan Graphics

Table of Contents

Introduction

RAKESH KHANNA AND MISHA MICHAEL

"So, what's it all about, this book?" asked the agent. She was trying hard not to look nervous. It was mostly working.

The burly man in the gold silk shirt leaned towards her, his elbows on the table, one hand cupped in the other. "It's a collection of seven horror stories. By seven different Indian authors," he said.

"Well, they're not all horror, not exactly," said the thinner man, standing at his side. He wore a black veshti and black fishnet sleeves and kohl around his eyes, and he gesticulated a lot as he spoke. "Some are just strange. They are strange and horrible tales."

"Okay," said the agent. "But what about this creature on the cover? What *is* a Bandigoat? They didn't tell me a lot about this mission, okay. They said it was safer not to know before I came here."

"They were probably right," said the thinner man, nodding.

"The ideal situation," said the burly man, slowly and deliberately, "is to have a large number of people on your side that you trust completely; but each person should know only a small part of the plan."

"No gods, no masters, no masterminds," said the thinner man, grinning.

The agent made herself grin back, but her brain was buzzing. She thought about her mission. She thought about trust. She thought about ideal situations. She thought about gods and demons, about masters and the people that masters enslaved. She thought about racists and semantic nihilists and war profiteers and misanthropic accelerationist lunatics. She thought about serial killers and suicide cults. She thought about panipuri and paneer soda and rainbow unicorns. She thought about neustonic life and gibberish meditation and pulsars and quasicrystals and Escher sentences. *More people have impossible dreams than I do.*

She blinked her eyes. "Come to the Bandigoat, please," she said.

The thinner man gesticulated. "You are familiar with the animal called a bandiCOOT, right? The bandicoot rat we have here in India? Did you know that the name comes from Telugu? *Pandikokku*, they call it. 'Pig-rat'. Twice the size of a normal rat. The British couldn't say the name correctly. Bandicoot it became.

"Well, once there was a little girl who was born outside the country. When she was still young, her family moved back here, to Chennai. Late one night, while she was looking out her window, she noticed something scary-looking moving through the garden shrubs outside her house. But she only saw it half in shadow; she couldn't glimpse its face. Then she heard it scratching, trying to get into the house under the door, and she cried out in alarm. Some adults came and chased the thing away, and she heard them call it a bandiGOAT—because in a Tamil accent, a *ka* sound becomes a *ga* sound, you know? And so she imagined this creature with the head of a goat and the claws and tail of a rat. And she imagined it growing very very big—as big as a person."

"Also, glowing green," the burly man cut in.

"Yes! And when she was imagining all that, there must have been some sort of entity hanging around nearby in the æther, waiting. And that entity could sense the little girl's ball of imagination and fascination and fear, and it caught hold of it, and inhabited it, and filled it with its power. And that's how the Bandigoat became real." He mimed a little explosion with his hands.

"Then what happened?" asked the agent. "Did the entity eat her?"

The thin man looked offended. "The Bandigoat isn't evil."

"She's more like a… guide," said the burly man. "To other places."

"She helps you travel time through your dreams. Or into other peoples' nightmares."

"Which is what's happening here," said the burly man, tapping the book that lay on the table between them. "Seven different strange and horrible dreams, by seven different dreamers."

The agent picked up the book and turned it over in her hands. She flipped through the pages. She read the table of contents. She closed the book and looked at the creature on the cover again.

Then she looked back up at the two men, who were both staring at her expectantly.

"So if I decide that I trust you," she asked, "how do I start?"

"Open the book," said the thin man.

"Don't think twice," said the burly man.

Then they said in unison, "Blink thrice."

The agent re-opened the book to the first story. She blinked her eyes once, and then twice, and again.

Funeral for a Demon

Srividya Tadepalli

There was not a cloud in sight on the afternoon they found Sarasu's body, though the rain lashed around them. After hours of searching, they found her about a kilometre from her house, close to a small pond bursting with water for the first time in years. Despite the rain, her body was bone dry. Three men, her sons, stepped carefully around that observation and then around her body as they picked her up and took her home.

They grew up hearing the rumours about their mother, and they learned to ignore as much as they could. The blind priestess at their village temple told the story of the *ibuyi* to all the children who bothered to visit. The *ibuyi* were twelve warrior demons who each served as patron saints of the hungry, the wronged, the persecuted, the battered, the neglected, the displaced, the homeless, the itinerant, the mad, the silenced, the unfree, and the labouring. The priestess had declared a long time ago with certainty that Sarasu was the twelfth of these demons, a protector of the worker.

Sarasu's sons walked together in silence now, carrying their mother as they mourned her, demon or not.

•

Sarasu had given her children strict instructions a week before she died. Four villages had to be fed on the twelfth day from the afternoon her body was carried through her village. She wanted to be buried only after this feast. They expected the body to decay and smell, but Sarasu smelled only of chamanthis for twelve days after her death.

The food was to be prepared inside the dead woman's house, as custom required. Outside, three buffaloes, three goats, three pigs, and three chickens were waiting to be slaughtered and cooked by three daughters of the house, all three daughters-in-law.

Preparations began in the dark hours just past midnight on the morning of the twelfth day. Relatives had already started arriving and moving towards the kitchen. Children were woken up and sent off to play. Sleepy festivity surrounded the house though it was death that had summoned everyone there.

Inside, Sasi and Paapa, the middle and youngest daughters-in-law, sat with other women from their family, grinding, peeling, cutting, and kneading. The oldest daughter-in-law, Jeyanthi, was outside making phone calls and arrangements. Their husbands sat under a tree behind the house with other men from the family, drinking late into the night and then early into the morning.

As the sky got pinker, the women made their way outside to watch Sasi slice into twelve necks one after the other with her sickle. The animals were carried off to be cleaned and prepared, and the women went back to their tasks.

A few minutes later, everyone, men included, hurried outside to the sound of Paapa's scream. All twelve animals looked back at them, untouched and alive.

The men laughed. Babu, Sasi's husband, picked up the sickle, still wet with blood, and slaughtered all the animals again. This time, the men cleaned and cut and picked and prepared, laughing through the grief at this unexpected bounty of flesh.

But then it happened again. And again. And by the fifth set of animals, Jeya, Sasi, and Paapa declared it a miracle. "The gods smile down on us," Ravi agreed. Paapa rapped her husband on his head with her knuckles. "Gods? Ha! This is the work of our demon."

•

As the women cooked, they told stories about Sarasu's generosity. Indira recalled how she regularly cooked for people around the village, taking oily, tasty treats to women who had just given birth or had just lost their mother. She would sometimes include some of her homemade medicinal teas and pastes accompanied by elaborate, specific instructions.

Paapa's seven-year-old son, Billa, cut in, "I saw her spit into the medicines she made! No, really, once I saw her crying into the mortar too!" The women laughed at sweet Billa, refusing to wonder aloud whether or not the story was true.

Outside, the men were laying out bedsheets for people to sit on so the feast could begin. Velu said, as he set out the banana leaves for the first row, "Sarasamma gave me money to take Muthu to Vizag and pay his college fees. The day we got news of his admission, we were arguing about whether he could go or not, and she showed up with some food, handed my wife the money, and insisted she was only paying her back for a loan she'd taken from us." It went without saying that poor Velu could never have ever lent anyone any money.

•

Those attending the feast, regardless of how long they were travelling, merely had to tell their employers that Sarasu had died. Any further explanation was neither given nor sought. Though some employers grumbled and muttered under their breath, Sarasu was feared widely enough by those of their classes and castes that no one complained.

There was one poor soul who had either not heard or not heeded this unspoken warning. A moneylender, not poor by any definition other than with regard to the fate that awaited him, decided it was a good day to harass Ravi about money he owed. The moneylender arrived with his band of men outside Sarasu's house just as people began to sit down to eat. Conversations came to an end abruptly as people recognized the man who managed to make the worst periods of their lives somehow worse. He bellowed, "Ravi! You bastard! You have money to feed all these morons but you don't have money to pay me back? Why don't you come here and we can arrange some entertainment for your guests, hmm?" The air was thick with fear and the moneylender revelled in it, not understanding whom the fear was for. Some of the older women tried to intervene, asking him to come back another day, but they were mocked and pushed around. Ravi hid inside the house with his furious wife. Paapa couldn't believe her husband was allowing that arrogant man to threaten her family while her mother-in-law's body lay less than 20 feet away.

As Paapa decided enough was enough and tore her way out of the house, violent coughs filled the air. The moneylender began to vomit: bile at first, then blood, then blood clots, looking soft as butter but blacker than the night. Paapa reached the moneylender just as the coughing man's mouth opened wider and wider, held ajar by two hands emerging from inside his body. The thugs who had accompanied him scattered in terror. The moneylender's jaw cracked, allowing it to open wide enough for a man with a sunken face to climb out. As the man stepped into the puddle of bile and blood, the moneylender fell to the ground, the skin around his throat sagging like a giant pelican's beak.

The new man, covered in saliva and other body fluids, looked around him, taking in the place of his birth. He made his way slowly towards Sarasu as the crowd parted for him. On reaching Sarasu, he bowed and then removed the bedsheet covering her body (Babu slapped a hand to

Sasi's mouth to stop her from saying anything), using it to cover himself as he walked away from the village gathering.

As Sasi managed to push Babu's hand away from her mouth, her own mother held her arm firmly in warning. "Don't, foolish girl. That's a *dhurindu*; let it go on its way. A demon like that is born from the flesh of greed once every 87 years. Your grandmother saw one too as a child."

Sasi and her co-sisters had always believed the rumours about Sarasu. During Sasi's wedding to Babu, the old priestess, who was actually her grand-aunt, told her she was the luckiest woman in the world to be able to call an *ibuyi* her mother-in-law.

She and Paapa stood together now looking at the moneylender, both unsure about whether they felt anger, pity, or relief. His eyes were missing, as were his gums and teeth. Only black, gaping holes remained in their place.

•

As guests began to eat, they talked about how fiercely Sarasu protected people, even strangers, and how she loved children the most. Sai was eight years old when she felt the full force of Sarasu's love. In between mouthfuls now, fifteen years later, she told her story. "I hated going to school, and my parents could never understand why. I didn't tell them how I was made to wash the toilets and sweep the floors as the rest of my classmates sat in the classroom. The teacher was nice to me sometimes, but the principal would slap me even when I answered his questions correctly.

"One afternoon, on my way back from school, Sarasammamma saw me crying and held me tight without asking any questions. The next day, when I got to school, everyone was standing outside the toilet, watching as a woman wound her snake-like arms around the principal so tightly that we could hear the bones crack. She had climbed out of the toilet, it seemed, and once she was satisfied with how many bones had been broken, she descended slowly back into the toilet with the principal still in her arms. I could see the principal's toes moving frantically as his body disappeared headfirst into that small hole. A new principal joined us later and he was shocked when he saw me sweeping the floor. He told me I never had to do that again." Sai's mother ate beside her and listened to this story for the first time with wet eyes.

On the other side of the house, a group of women began washing the cooking vessels. Mangamma from two streets away recalled the time a Reddy from the neighbouring village had tried to strike her in the middle of his paddy field during a harvest. Sarasu, who was working next to her at the time, somehow made her way in the blink of an eye to the space between Mangamma and the Reddy. She yelled an obscenity at the man (the recounting of which made Mangamma and everyone else laugh), and the Reddy froze. Mangamma swore that he literally stopped moving. They rushed away then, and heard the next day that he had died of a heart attack in his sleep.

The men who finished eating gathered under a tree to play some cards. They were the same group that had to carry the moneylender's broken body to bury along the railway tracks. They played in silence for a while, and then Sami couldn't help himself. He said, "She didn't believe in letting families handle their own business. I used to hate her for it. You remember the time my first wife left me? Sarasattha walked into our home one time unannounced, and saw me beating Kala. She screamed and pinched my ear and yelled at me. I agreed in the end that I would not raise my hand anymore, and Kala cried and accepted my apology. I was young and stupid, and it happened again. But this time, Kala became frighteningly calm, packed my things, and threw me out of the house.

"Later, when Swathi and I got married, Sarasattha visited us. She brought us food and made us promise that we would never treat each other with unkindness or cruelty. It was a difficult thing to swallow, this old woman telling me how I could and could not treat my wife, but I don't plan to cross her even though she's dead." Sami shuddered. The older men in the circle mumbled in agreement while the younger men looked on thoughtfully in silence.

•

Once the children had all eaten two helpings of each of the four meat dishes, Malli—Ragul and Jeyanthi's daughter—led a small army of them towards Sarasu's body. The children were morbidly curious, as children often are. They wanted to see what a dead body looked like, whether it was still Sarasu, whether they could catch a small twitch of muscle or heave of chest.

Trying to convince them that death was not something to be afraid of, Malli found herself walking with exaggerated confidence towards her grandmother's body. Her grandmother was now barely covered by her mother's dupatta after the bedsheet had been stolen by the strange man. She slowed as she got closer to the head of the body, and then gently pulled the dupatta off. Chamanthis were growing now from her dead grandmother's eyes and mouth. She stood silent and unshaken as the other children ran back shrieking to report what they had discovered to their parents.

•

The stories that the women, sitting amongst themselves, told about Sarasu were slightly different. Everyone knew Sarasu had no interest in men. She had arrived in their village for the first time some 40 years ago, not speaking Telugu or any other language from the region. She found her partner in Chamanthi soon after. They raised Chamanthi's triplets together. No one knew who the father was, and no one thought it wise to press the issue.

Chamanthi died a few years before Sarasu did, and Sarasu had arranged for a grand celebration in her memory. At the end of that night, once the men had drunk themselves to sleep, by design it seemed, the women gathered around Sarasu as she recited the story of their life together as though she was reading from a book of poetry. These stories were gentle and full of love, they were unvarnished and full of sex, and all of them were eye-opening to the young women in the circle who hadn't yet discovered what they deserved—and could demand—in life and in love.

As the stories of that day were recounted now, Malli listened, seeing her grandmother, and herself, in a new light as things fell into place.

•

The family now gathered around Sarasu, with all the visitors forming a larger circle around them at a respectful distance. They planned to lay her down in her own garden, where Chamanthi was also buried. As her sons approached to carry her away, they noticed moths on her feet. They watched as moths landed gently on her face, her arms, her torso, covering her hair and her nails. They kept coming, in beautiful blurs of yellows, blues, and reds, and nobody dared move. No one could see Sarasu beneath the many-coloured wings. A cool breeze swept past everyone gathered there under the sky that day, and the moths flew up to greet it. Not a sound was heard, not a breath was taken. Sarasu's body was gone.

The silence was broken by Malli's giggle, shy and low at first, and then full-throated, thigh-slapping laughter. And slowly, everyone joined her. The chamanthis in the garden were in full bloom.

The Lucy Temerlin Institute for Broken Shapeshifters Resident #11: ChestPain Sumitra

Kuzhali Manickavel

Every year, the northeast monsoon hides the Lucy Temerlin Institute for Broken Shapeshifters in a cocoon of rain and impenetrable grey mist. The residents shiver and Sister Georgina moves like an impending disaster through the halls, the pallu of her sari pulled firmly over one shoulder. Girls shuffle wearily to the mess hall and glut themselves from large, steaming buckets of upma or idlies. After that, there is nothing left to do but shuffle back to their metal cots and curl up under thin blankets. The lucky ones fall asleep. The others simply stare at the grey light trickling in through the blanket and wonder why they are always here, like this.

That particular year was worse than usual. There had already been one flood and the more stubborn corridors were refusing to release their floodwater. Sister Georgina tried to make the residents drain them but most refused, and those who did volunteer were swallowed up by the more dangerous parts of the institute.

ChestPain Sumitra had enthusiastically volunteered to help, then stayed in bed wrapped in her blanket, eyes shut, telling herself she was already asleep. Like most of the residents here, ChestPain Sumitra did not matter. She always gorged herself on white rice and overripe bananas, and she always sat at the same place in the mess. Sometimes she read Tamil pulp magazines after lunch, and once she had wandered out into the rain for no reason. Otherwise she was as unremarkable as everyone else. She had a mild, garden-variety shapeshifting issue of turning into a decaying horse's corpse when she sneezed very hard. The shift only lasted a few hours, and was more of an inconvenience than anything else; she had no treatment regime and whenever she did shift, she was tossed into one of the smaller Containment Chambers until she shifted back. The staff often forgot about her, but ChestPain Sumitra didn't mind; the chambers were comfortable and had small windows which were just clean enough to let in a weak stream of grey light. She had stopped getting mail and visitors many years ago, and nobody could remember why she was called ChestPain Sumitra. She was one of the legion of residents who nobody knew existed. Which is why even decades after the incident occurred, no one understood why it happened to her, of all people. Perhaps there had been something about her that no one knew, something special and mysterious. But this seemed highly unlikely.

That had also been the year of badly-behaved cyclones. Large groups of them were settling on the roof of the institute and Sister Georgina was sure that cyclones were not supposed to do that. Clouds crowded onto the tops of trees, and the sky was full of dark grey heaviness. The institute was quiet and bare. Sister Georgina sat in her room, humming to herself, while the girls huddled on their metal beds, waiting for whatever was going to happen. Many of them had already stopped coming down for meals, remaining in their blankets and breathing slowly, like they were hibernating.

ChestPain Sumitra curled up under her thin blanket, wondering if there was something special one had to do to hibernate like the others. They didn't look comfortable, but they were completely still, and ChestPain Sumitra found this deeply moving. She imagined it was like falling asleep and waking among unfamiliar flowers and stinging insects. Or maybe nothing happened at all. You fell asleep and then you just didn't exist and that was it.

One afternoon, ChestPain Sumitra actually fell asleep while huddled inside her blanket. She didn't dream, but she remembered that when she first came to the institute, she loved pretending that she had chest pain. She would put one hand on her chest, slowly collapse her shoulders forward, and close her eyes. Then she would fall—sometimes to the floor, and one time all the way down a set of stairs. Concerned voices arched over her in a canopy while hands held her—so, so many hands—like she was something precious. Someone would touch her face and ChestPain Sumitra's heart would flutter very faintly. But the girls quickly tired of her. Soon she was falling to the floor, utterly alone, and nobody even noticed.

ChestPain Sumitra slept deeply until four o'clock and woke with a start, worried that she was going to miss her tiffin. She could smell something being deep fried in oil. She was so focussed on getting to the mess that she even forgot to wear her chappals. Which was probably why she didn't notice the murder hornets either, even though they were already pouring out of her palm by then.

•

At first she thought they were flowers. Hornets were swarming lazily about her head and landing on her face, but for some reason they seemed like petals, pale and slightly curled, so fresh and firm you could snap them in two. It was only when she was in the mess, grabbing large handfuls of vadas, that she saw that they were hornets. There was no blood and it didn't hurt. ChestPain Sumitra thought this was strange. Murder hornets coming out of the palm of your hand seemed like something that should be extremely painful.

At the other end of the mess hall, a girl with a bobcut sat stooped over her tiffin. Otherwise, the mess was completely empty. ChestPain Sumitra wondered if she should warn Bobcut about the hornets. She should definitely tell Sister Georgina, she knew that. And she was definitely going to do that later, after she finished her vadas. But it seemed like it was already too late to say anything to Bobcut. What would be the good of saying *watch out for the murder hornets* seconds before the hornets attacked? ChestPain Sumitra decided that if she had been Bobcut, she would not want to know. A few of the murder hornets were already starting to fly off, lazily heading towards Bobcut's bent head. Soon a steady stream was headed towards her, settling on her back, arms, and head. But she didn't seem to notice.

"Excuse me please," said ChestPain Sumitra, standing up. "Excuse me."

But then there was such a scream of pain and hopelessness that ChestPain Sumitra froze. The hornets were either consuming or burrowing into Bobcut—whatever it was, it was angry and violent and seemed to go on for a very long time. At first ChestPain Sumitra hoped someone would come, but it soon became clear that even if someone did come, there was nothing they could do. Bobcut was mostly gone anyway, except for one leg and her hair. Finally, the hornets began drifting back to ChestPain Sumitra, landing on her shoulders and arms. She walked over to where Bobcut had been. On the table were the remains of a vada and a tumbler of tea with a dark brown skin stretched over it. Hundreds of dead hornets lay scattered over the floor and table. The only thing that remained of the girl was half of a bloody tooth.

•

Sister Georgina's heart was unpredictable. Sometimes she fell desperately in love with a resident, showering them with an inappropriate, motherly affection that had absolutely no boundaries. Sometimes she developed a deep and intense hatred for one of the girls for no reason, relentlessly terrorizing them until the girl had no choice but to bury herself deep inside the walls of the institute. But she regarded ChestPain Sumitra as more of an unpleasant surprise. She disliked being reminded that ChestPain Sumitra existed, and most of the time treated her as completely invisible.

Whenever ChestPain Sumitra tried to talk to her, Sister Georgina's hooded eyes went to her ledger or lingered on some passing resident she loved or hated. Once the good sister had simply walked away while ChestPain Sumitra was in mid-sentence.

Which was why everything was so difficult now. ChestPain Sumitra was standing in Sister Georgina's room, a steady stream of hornets pouring out of her greasy, vada-scented hand, as she tried to explain that Bobcut had just been killed in the mess by murder hornets.

"What is all this," said Sister Georgina peevishly. "Who are you? I mean what *is* all this?"

For the fourth time, ChestPain Sumitra explained what had happened.

"But what is the *meaning* of it all?" insisted Sister Georgina. "Why are all these bees in here?"

"They're murder hornets."

"Oh fuck off."

ChestPain Sumitra stretched out her other hand, revealing the broken tooth. Sister Georgina rolled her eyes.

"Why are you bringing me all this?" she said, completely exasperated.

ChestPain Sumitra took a deep breath and told her story yet again. This time, Sister Georgina listened. Then she covered her face with her hands, and told ChestPain Sumitra to get out.

By now, the hornets were roaming the institute in small swarms, independent of ChestPain Sumitra. They had overpowered some of the smaller residents and kept disrupting the electricity. ChestPain Sumitra was sent to collect her blanket, toothbrush, and her bar of Hamam soap. Then she was taken to the Seclusion Pods. Like many parts of the institute, the Pods had never been used; they were obscenely expensive, and no one knew what to do with them. The usual Containment Chambers were currently filled with heavy cardboard boxes which Sister Georgina was too scared to open. So a Seclusion Pod would have to make do for now. After walking for nearly an hour, they finally arrived at a large steel sphere that seemed to be hovering above the ground. Sister Georgina gave ChestPain Sumitra a small shove inside, quickly locked the door, and left.

The Pod had a bed—not a rusty metal cot, but an actual wooden bed with a very comfortable mattress. There was a small bathroom, an air conditioner, and a fridge filled with unhealthy processed food. There was also a television set that played an unending stream of Doordarshan Tamil dramas. For the first few days, ChestPain Sumitra ate, slept and watched TV. She gorged herself on thick potato chips, cold, hard chocolate, and Limca. She also spent a lot of time watching the hornets. They liked to hover in the corners of the Pod or nestle inside her scanty hair. A lot of them just lay around in small piles. They were not dead; they were just being perfectly still, and ChestPain Sumitra thought this was incredibly sad and beautiful.

She could no longer tell when her shapeshifts were going to happen. Usually, there was an aura of unnecessarily dramatic body contortions and the smell of gasoline in her mouth. Now, her shapeshifts kept catching her off-guard. Suddenly, she would feel like her body was slowly tearing in two. Her mouth and nose seemed to seal up and there was a dry, hard knocking sound from somewhere near her feet. Then, a dry, cold silence until the shift reversed and dissolved.

For a while, ChestPain Sumitra tried to be concerned about all this. She told herself that hornets were not supposed to come out of her palm. They were not supposed to just lie there like they were depressed. Her shapeshifts were not supposed to be like this. She probably wasn't supposed to shapeshift at all—she wasn't sure about that, though. In the end, being concerned turned out to be a lot harder than it looked, and she eventually gave up.

•

The layers of cyclones continued to push into the institute, rumbling loudly against the walls. Clouds were seeping into the rooms and nobody could see a thing. Many residents who had ventured to the mess hall or the bathroom never returned. To make things worse, the hornets were still roaming the halls and attacking girls. They had even carried away a small girl in an oversized yellow nightie. It had happened very slowly and no one had stepped in to help, though several residents had watched with great concern. It was only when a moderate-sized swarm of hornets settled on Sister Georgina's chin and attempted to consume her mouth that the murder hornets were finally considered a real problem.

"How long can this go on ma?" asked Sister Georgina with righteous indignation. She was sitting in ChestPain Sumitra's Pod. The attack had left a small forest of warts on her upper lip, but that was it.

"They took Bhanumathi," said Sister Georgina. "They just flew away with her and nobody did anything. You know Bhanumathi?"

"No."

"I also don't know. Apparently she was very small."

"Why didn't anyone help?"

"How should I know? No civic sense. Stupid fellows."

Sister Georgina had no real interest in Bhanumathi. She was too offended by the fact that the hornets had attacked *her*, Sister Georgina, instead of one of the residents. She believed this was how the fight for Indian Independence had begun. Sister Georgina did not like Indian Independence, because she was enamoured by the idea of being ruled by white people.

"I think we can cut off your hand," she said to ChestPain Sumitra. "If there is no hand then what will the bees do?"

"What if they move to my other hand? What if they never go away?"

Sister Georgina watched the hornets lazily wend their way from one end of the Seclusion Pod to the other. ChestPain Sumitra realised that even if the hornets did go away, Sister Georgina would probably want to cut off her hands anyway.

•

The next day, ChestPain Sumitra noticed something sticking out of the skin of her palm. She pulled at it, first absent-mindedly, then in a more focussed way as it continued to spill out of her skin. It seemed to be a very long knot of hair, and at the end of it was a giant hornet. It was the size of a kitten and had an old, broken face that quivered, like it was on the verge of tears. Hair was wrapped around its legs and thorax, and its wings were black. Some of the other, smaller hornets hovered over it for a few seconds and flew off, as if it didn't concern them.

ChestPain Sumitra kept the hornet on her pillow, with the long tail of hair wrapped snugly around it. She tried feeding it jam but could not figure out how to do so. She finally smeared it all over its broken, quivering face, but the hornet simply lay there, breaking ChestPain Sumitra's heart.

Meanwhile, the multiple cyclones outside had finally caused flooding that was breaking past the corridors and entering the other parts of the institute. There were rumours that the floodwater had even had the audacity to enter Sister Georgina's room. Not only were residents going missing, they were being found again, in places that were usually reserved for staff and Sister Georgina. Bhanumathi was discovered swimming in one of the corridors, looking so well-nourished and healthy that no one recognized her.

One afternoon, when ChestPain Sumitra was standing at her window and watching the floodwater, she saw Sister Georgina walk by, dragging two girls behind her by the scruffs of their nighties. The girls looked morose and disappointed, but were very beautiful. ChestPain Sumitra suddenly thought of her parents. She thought of what it must have been like to see their small daughter shapeshift for the first time, finally ending up as a rotting horse's corpse. And then to have her shapeshift back again—maybe that just made everything even worse. For the first time in her life, ChestPain Sumitra felt sorry for her parents. But it wasn't a very strong feeling, and it passed quickly.

•

The next time Sister Georgina passed by her Pod, ChestPain Sumitra asked her to open the door. She expected Sister Georgina to ignore her and walk away, but to her surprise the preoccupied sister unlocked the door and disappeared down the hall. For a few seconds, ChestPain Sumitra did not know what to do. She looked at the bed, littered with empty chip packets and plastic soda bottles. She looked at the piles of hornets on the floor, and the large hornet lying sadly on her pillow. It made much more sense to stay here. Not just for now, but for however long she had to continue living.

With the giant murder hornet draped across her shoulders, ChestPain Sumitra left the Pod and walked down the hall with a dense cloud of hornets following her. She stopped to help groups of girls get back to the relatively dry mess hall. She pulled small, drowning girls out of the water and held them for a while, marvelling at how light they were. In the evening, someone saw her wading into a flooded hallway, towards something they couldn't see. That was the last time anyone saw her.

•

Hornets still roam the corridors of the institute, swarming and attacking residents at random or carrying away the smaller ones. Sometimes the hornets fall down in mid-flight, landing on the floor with a small tap. They just lie there and never move again, even though they aren't dead.

The Mirror of the Mung

LUNGMYING LEPCHA

The flock of sheep cried from the far end of the hill. The day was dying. After a heavy downpour, the clouds started to make their way out towards the horizon, and the light of the moon prevailed.

Adon, a seventeen-year-old youth with deeply tanned skin, was returning home along a rugged, slippery path through the local forest where he had gone to fetch firewood.

He was afraid that someone was following behind him, and he guessed that it might be Muloon Mung. Adon had heard the story recently from his sixty-year-old grandfather, Ambi Thyung, of how a shopkeeper from nearby Kabi village had vanished in the middle of the daytime. The man had informed his family that he would be in the shop; but when his wife called him later on for his lunch, he was nowhere to be found. It wasn't until Ambi Thyung—who happened to be the *bongthing*, or chief shaman of the area—was summoned for inspection that the truth was learned: the shopkeeper had been taken by the Muloon Mung.

Later that very evening, the shopkeeper had returned home, only to tell his family how Muloon Mung had tricked him by coming to the door in the guise of his wife, and then taken him into the jungle and eaten his soul.

As soon as he had finished his story, the man fell to the ground dead.

For this is what is known about Muloon Mung: he always lets his victims return home, to survive just long enough to tell the tale of how they vanished.

The cicadas sang a lullaby to Adon as he made his way over the last bridge spanning the Rongyoung River and crossed into Labi, his native village. Fireflies flickered around him, lighting his way through the darkness. He had neglected to carry his mobile phone—he had left it charging, being overly optimistic that he would return before sunset. But his plan had changed when he found a patch of *ashilo*—the local raspberries—on top of a hill, and spent time picking them.

Crack—he heard a sudden noise. Adon was frightened, but strove to remain calm. Like a warning bell, the thought rang in his mind: *a weak heart gives power to evil spirits.*

Adon turned to look behind him and saw Anum Angha, the thirty-year-old local drunkard famous for his crooked-toothed smile. He had fallen at the base of a *sumbryang* tree.

"*Ayya!*" Anum Angha cried from the ground. "Who put this tree in my way? I didn't see it—and I'm sure I've never seen it here before. Ah! Adon! It's you… coming back from collecting firewood, are you? Come, let's go back together!"

Adon was quite relieved to have a companion. They walked the rest of the way home talking about the upcoming village fair and the grand feast they would all have.

•

The sun had set, and darkness prevailed in the village of Labi. A small fire was burning near the gate of Adon's home.

Ambi Thyung—or Ambi Ajo*, as he was sometimes called—was out in their kitchen garden searching for some local coriander to garnish his favorite bamboo-shoot soup.

Just then Adon arrived, along with Anum Angha. Ambi Ajo was surprised to see Anum Angha, and invited him to stay for dinner.

"Tell me, Angha," said Ambi Thyung, "how is your work going on? Are you getting enough wood for the village fire, or are you drunk all day at Anue Asha's shop?" He let out a hearty laugh to temper the sting of his words.

"I'm working, Thyung! But due to the monsoon season, my work has slowed down, you know. Days become dull and dreary with the heavy fog… and I am scared of running into Muloon Mung."

"Oh yes, yes!" agreed Ambi Thyung. "You must be very careful. Last time I was making my way through the woods, on the way to a nearby village to treat a fever, I heard a strange, loud whistling sound. I prayed very hard to Ithbu Rum, and was saved when the village people came to get me. I thought I would die that day!"

"*Apuii!*" exclaimed Anum Angha. "Thyung, I am glad you returned safely. There are so many *mungsong* about. I wonder how, in the old days, Thyung Punchuwang managed to put up with them. That poor old man—he lost his wife to the mungsong."

Adon had always been intrigued by stories of the mungsong—especially the tales of Muloon Mung, who was known for haunting the Lepcha villagers in his area. Although most of the village children were too scared to listen to such stories, Adon was a brave one; after all, he was next in line to become bongthing after his grandfather. He had lost his parents in an accident—an accident which was said to have been caused by a mung.

---

* *Thyung* means "grandfather" or "old man" in Lepcha; *Ajo* means the same in the Sikkimese common tongue.

"Anum," said Adon, "please tell me the story of Thyung Punchuwang, please? I want to know more."

"*Ayuu!* You shouldn't say his name—you're still young," said Anum Angha. "I don't even want to risk telling the story myself—who knows if I'll get a chance to see the sun tomorrow! Thyung, you're the one with the powers. Please tell this child. I guess we *should* tell him, so that he's aware of such things, and knows how to escape them."

Before starting his story, Ambi Thyung chanted a few prayers for their safety. Then he began.

"So listen," he said. "We really shouldn't talk about the mungsong at all, because they are always listening to us, and we shouldn't give them any opportunity to attack our souls. But if you stay quiet, it should be alright. If you have any questions, just speak them quickly; don't hold them in your head for too long. If you even think of a mung too much, it can appear to you, no matter where you may be at the time.

"The word *muloon* means 'shape-shifting'—the power to change into anything. And *mung*, of course, is the word for any sort of ghost or evil power.

"Ren Punchuwang was a great and renowned bongthing of our community. Many stories are told about his life—especially about his encounters with Muloon Mung.

"One such story goes like this.

"Ren Punchuwang lived with his wife at the bottom of this hill, quite far off, on the outskirts of the village. It was the summer season and the cicadas around his home were making a lot of noise. It was so loud and irritating that he couldn't sleep at night.

"The insects kept up their racket for almost a week until Ren Punchuwang couldn't bear it any more. One day he said to his wife, '*Nyom*, I'm going to the jungle to find those cicadas and kill them. Cook some rice—don't bother making anything else. I will bring the cicadas and we can eat them for our dinner.'

"Saying this, Ren Punchuwang went into the forest, holding a torch made from a bundle of sticks that he had tied together and set alight.

"His wife watched him from their window. After a while she saw a huge blaze of fire from deep in the forest, and she assumed that her husband had done the job.

"The fire kept blazing, and she watched until she saw a figure coming towards her home, silhouetted against the flames. The figure appeared to be carrying something under its arm, like a small log.

"Then she looked more carefully, and what she saw made her eyes bulge out.

"She rushed to the store room and pulled out all the firewood they had gathered for the whole winter. She piled the logs in her doorway and set them on fire to block the entrance. Then she heard the sound of something coming up to the house.

"It was the Muloon Mung, and in his hands he was holding one of Ren Punchuwang's thighs. He stuck it through the ventilator over the door and said, '*Punchuwang tah tah!*'—Look, there's Punchuwang!

"The mung knew he wouldn't be able to pass through the flames. So he waited outside, peeking into the ventilator now and then to check on the brightness of the fire.

"He was waiting for the fire to die down, you see, so he could get into the home.

"And indeed, once all the logs had burned up, the Muloon Mung went inside and gobbled up Punchuwang's wife, too.

"It's a pretty gory story. But it's true."

"So tell us, Thyung," said Adon, who had been listening with rapt attention, "where is Thyung Punchuwang now?"

"Well, they all say he was reborn," said Ambi Thyung, "since he had the power to come back to life; but his wife had no such power.

"You know old Punchuwang Thyung, who lives on the other side of this hill. He is the one, the reincarnation of Ren Punchuwang, the bongthing of old. But hardly anyone approaches him anymore, for the fear of meeting Muloon Mung.

"Because the mungsong *do* visit him sometimes, you know. I, too, visited him once, to discuss the rituals to be performed at the village *rumfaat*."

"Well," said crooked-toothed Anum Angha, "my sister and my nephew were taken by Muloon Mung too, you know."

"I'm sorry, Anum," said Adon.

"No, no, don't you be sorry. It was their own ill luck that brought their end."

"Anum, if you don't mind," said Adon, "could you please tell me how it happened?"

"It happened about a decade back," said Anum Angha. "It was the harvest season, Dzo Tyum. Normit, my sister, was planning to go to her fields to harvest the ripened rice. She asked Kingchum, her fourteen-year-old son, to stay back home and study for his exams.

"Before leaving, she warned him that he shouldn't open the door for anyone other than his mother, and that he should definitely not go anywhere with anyone else.

"Just an hour after Normit left, Kingchum was mopping the floor of their home when he was called outside by his mother. Except—people say that *this* Normit looked quite a bit chubbier than she had when she had left. There was something different about her!

"But when she called her son, he went to her, and they both went off somewhere.

"In the evening, when the real Normit came back home, she was surprised not to find her son. She wasn't sure what had happened until she heard a cry from far away—'Amu, amu, save me!'—and looked out to see. At the far end of the hill, she saw her son running towards her, and not far behind him was the Muloon Mung.

"She quickly gathered her wits and started to build a fire at their doorstep.

"She took her son in, and then fanned the flames and waited, praying patiently to god; but it was in vain. Because Muloon Mung took them after the fire had died down.

"Ever since then, Muloon Mung is feared a lot. We are not safe even in our own homes."

"That's enough for today," said Ambi Thyung. "Let's not speak more. Angha, would you like to spend the night here, or return back home?"

"Obviously, Thyung, I would rather sleep here. If I go now, who knows if I'll get the chance to see the sun tomorrow."

"Fine, fine," said Thyung. "Adon, help Anum with the bed. You two can sleep together in the hall."

"Yes, Thyung," said Adon. "*Aryum sonap*—good night."

•

It was midnight. Adon was unable to sleep properly; he was experiencing a nightmare. He saw himself in a room full of Muloon Mungsong, and between them was the body of Thyung Punchuwang, which the mungsong were dismembering and serving for their meal.

•

The next morning, Adon left for his convent school, which was a little less than a kilometre's walk from his village. On the way, he met his best friend Denri, from Samdong village, waiting for him on the path.

They were both very excited: today was the last day of school, and the jollity of the start of summer vacation seemed to float on the cool breeze.

Since they were running a bit late, they decided to take a shortcut. Their alternate route led across the village *phool* over the Ramshing River. Here they had to be very cautious—not so much because of the river current, but because of the small burned-out cottage which sat on the other side, at the end of the phool, near the main road.

Adon read the slightly faded name written on the tin signboard hanging lopsided from the entrance: AUNTIE HAPPY LAMICHANEY CANTEEN—COME EAT AND RELAX.

Adon had heard his father talk about this place. He had heard the story of how Ambi Thyung had used his magic powers to defeat the Kaapaat practitioner who lived here, when the entire village had been slowly dying under the grip of his spell.

Although the villagers had gone back to their normal lives again, there were still rumours that the Kaapaat practitioner had not died, that he had actually only fled from this place to somewhere unknown. For there were still reports of people seeing strange shadows around the vicinity of the cottage, and of weak-hearted people falling terribly ill.

Adon and Denri spoke about these rumours in low voices as they passed the cottage. Denri related what he knew about Kaapaat, the black magic practice also known in Lepcha as *Nyung*. He told Adon about how when a person was affected by Kaapaat, their skin became jaundiced and yellow and their teeth began to break apart.

"They make offerings to the devil in return for prosperity. It's basically just that. My aunt told me that in her village, there was one house in which the people practiced Kaapaat. One day the whole family left on a sightseeing trip to visit the tourist places in South Sikkim. Only the grandmother and her granddaughter stayed home. It was the night of the full moon, when the offerings are supposed to be made; but since no one was home, no one came in for food, and there was nothing to offer. So instead, the grandmother offered her own granddaughter to the devil.

"It is said that the heart of a victim of Kaapaat turns to stone. That's why, during the funeral, the granddaughter's heart didn't burn at all. And now, they keep that stone in the house.

"There are other cases where a mother has even sacrificed her own son to the devil. This is a very evil sort of black magic; once you get into the business, there is no going back. Your entire family lineage will be eaten by the devil if you can't fulfill his demands."

Listening to these stories, Adon got chills. He was determined never to visit the places of Kaapaat. But as Denri explained it, the only way to know was from the bad energy a place gave off. That, and the fact that the food would become ice cold as soon as it was served—that was another indication that an establishment was practicing Kaapaat.

That evening, on the way back from school, Adon and Denri took the long main road to avoid the cottage, which was even eerier at night. Afterwards they split up, taking separate paths to their homes.

But then, as he was passing Anum Angha's home, he saw a huge fire blazing behind it. Loud cries filled the air. When he ventured closer, he found people rushing through the house busily, as though they were preparing for a rumfaat ceremony.

Adon stood outside, perplexed, until Ambi Thyung saw him. He immediately took his grandson inside the house, chanted some prayers, and fed him a mugwort leaf.

Bewildered by his grandfather's actions, Adon asked him what was wrong.

"Anum Angha has been captured by Muloon Mung," he said. "I tried my best to rescue him; but you know it's next to impossible to get a person back who has been captured by Muloon Mung. After a thorough search turned up nothing, he came back himself and told the story of how he'd been taken when he was on his way to the liquor shop."

From the far end of the kitchen, Adon heard the plaintive cries of Anum Angha's wife. "I had told him not to drink, not to get into such things!" she wailed. "If only we had shifted into town along with our children when they left the village, I wouldn't have lost him today!"

Adon listened, sighing, full of fear and uncertainty.

Note 1: It is said that Muloon Mung is still alive and active in the vicinity of villages such as Lingthem, and in the Upper and Lower Dzongu areas. Although they are not as common as in the olden days, a person with bad luck may still encounter them. Till now, no person who has met a Muloon Mung has ever escaped it. There is a superstition in our community that one mustn't ever fake one's identity, or pretend to be someone else—for no one knows; it might be Muloon Mung.

Note 2: This story is built on many real facts, but the characters and some of the place names are fictional.

Salt Slough

M. L. Krishnan

Maickelpatti, or the Abandonment of Safe Fishing Protocols in a Tamil Nadu Village

Dr. Kathirvel Selvan

Abstract

Further inland from the mouth of the Cauvery delta sits Maickelpatti, a nondescript village that once held an average population of eight hundred citizens. After the devastation wrought by Cyclone Bagha, which left an estimated 6500 dead in Tamil Nadu and over 8000 displaced, Maickelpatti served as an unfortunate microcosm of the enormity of the disaster. Rising floodwaters cleaved off a third of the village—destroying people, homes, and livelihoods. In an effort to make amends, the Tamil Nadu government planted thousands of mangroves over a period of two weeks to preserve what was left of the land. This brought in a heterogenous influx of faunal species to the lagoon, including milkfish, fiddler crabs, and several varieties of prawn. As a result, the greatly diminished population of Maickelpatti—now estimated to be three hundred citizens—took to fishing despite their lack of experience, given that their livelihoods pre-typhoon relied on a dependable, elephant yam crop. This paper argues that the unnatural-seeming deaths that occurred between the Tamil months of Thai and Maasi earlier this year were predicated on the reckless practices of a people unused to catamarans and commonsense fishing protocols[1].

I. Banana Prawn versus Snake Gourd

The people of Maickelpatti have historically engaged in elephant yam farming, with supplemental incomes from snake gourd cultivation on strips of vacant land trellised with gourd frames, and an illegal but flourishing arrack trade. Pazham—a fifth-generation snake gourd farmer—was one of the first documented *unnatural* deaths. One night, Pazham had borrowed a coracle from a friend and waded out into the lagoon in search of banana prawns. He had been drinking earlier that evening, and through hearsay, had concluded that fish glutted the backwaters every night[2]. If he had been successful in his fishing endeavor, a kilo of prawns would have netted him a tidy sum of Rs. 550, commensurate with market rates. Despite Pazham's weakness for arrack, he had been a fairly successful farmer and would have known that even his best crop would have netted him only Rs. 52.56 per kilo, compared to the banana prawns selling at ten times that rate. Given the facts, it can

1 I do not know how to say this, except to say I once believed this to be true. Now, I no longer know myself. Perhaps what I saw was my own failing—a scleral condition, bands of light pleating across my eyeball. But this is, of course, a lie.

2 Pazham drank with a group of four friends every night. It was said that he preferred their company to his wife, to his children, to his ailing granduncle. Their words held a heft that weighed Pazham down like a boulder, flattening what was left of his vertebrae. Two years ago, he had farmed yams because his friends had farmed yams as a passing fancy. He had stopped when they had stopped. And when they steered him toward this luminous, new enterprise of prawning, he followed suit.

thusly be concluded that Pazham's death[3] was attributed to his inebriated state[4], his lack of experience with the boat, and his underlying greed—as reconfirmed by the taluk police.

II. The Rigor of Roots

Baseless superstition has gripped the psyche of this village. While we have data to measure the physical devastation after Bagha, by what measure can we ascertain its psychological toll? It is therefore foreseeable that after the third *unnatural* death[5], the villagers began prostrating themselves to the mangrove, believing it to be sentient. This worshipful reverence[6] was echoed by almost everyone in Maickelpatti, who spoke of the trees as though they were close friends or loved ones that required emotional placation.

III. Bigg Boss

It is understood that a new skill cannot be mastered amid distractions. This was evident in the youth of Maickelpatti, who are all held hostage by the corrosive influence of *Bigg Boss*. Boys and girls roam about, their faces glued to phone screens. IG reels and WhatsApp groups are digital shrines to their two favorite contestants—the unkempt, C-grade

---

3 Everyone insisted that it was because Pazham was a drunken fool who beat his wife until her screams tore the night into ragged edges of sound. That it was only because of this. Because the violence that budded out of Pazham's own body was so unexplainable, it must have been a response from the lagoon.

4 I found Pazham floating amid the mangrove roots, his corpse pickled with salt. Chlorophyll wept out of his orifices as his stomach distended, the waters rippling green.

5 This was Guna, a toddy tapper. Here again, there are stories. Murmurs that Guna brought this all upon himself, that he was a child killer, that he murdered his own son. Another murmur about the son's love-marriage causing Guna's ruin. Was that not a betrayal that singed the blood, made it boil?

6 As they laid Guna's body on the shore, his mouth gaped open. His teeth were translucent, devoid of color. Already, bark threaded his veins. Already, leaves branched through ears. The villagers gently nudged Guna into the lagoon.

hero whose gloom breaks hearts; and the agreeable pornstar who also somehow embodies a demure bride. The youth cry over favoritism, injustices, and house rules. They vote furiously for their preferred candidates.

One such obsessed youth was Harini—a promising student preparing for the state board exams. Like her peers, Harini was also gripped by a debilitating *Bigg Boss* obsession. While the reason appeared indirect at best, it could be surmised that Harini's parents had pushed for her sudden marriage[7] to her maternal uncle[8] since her attention[9] had strayed in unproductive ways. The enthusiasm she had once shown in her studies had waned as a direct result of the TV program.

Conclusion

The aforementioned examples clearly indicate that Maickelpatti's current atmosphere of distraction[10] and malaise[11] does not foster skill-building, information acquisition, or progress in any field—be it farming or fishing. Thus, the only *unnatural*[12] demise[13] in this scenario is the villagers' entrepreneurial spirit in the aftermath of Cyclone Bagha, and not the haphazard mix of easily preventable deaths.

---

7 The wedding, the wedding! You should have been there. But maybe not. It probably was a fluke of kindness or luck that kept you away, and you must cherish it.

8 One moment, he is a man. When he walks up the pandal, he softens into macerated flesh as though he had been breathing water. A stench of rot and fish and bright green. Petals ripening out of hair follicles, the rim of his eye sockets, ears, feet. Now, a thicket of porous blooms move in his stead.

9 He, it, was beautiful. I might have stolen a flower in the ensuing chaos. I might have swallowed it whole. Please believe me when I tell you that I only wanted to learn.

10 I feel the urge to pincushion myself with the mangrove's roots.

11 Or void myself into a pneumatophore as an offering, a hymn.

12 I may be gone, marked as an *unnatural* death. But I want you to know that I was pliable and willing. To the waters, to its benthic floor. Even eager.

13 I want you to know that.

Cur

Miriam Kumaradoss-Hohauser

-1-

The Cur arrived in the neighbourhood a few months after I did. He drifted in like the clouds of ground-up cow dung and cement and god-knows-what-else that blew ceaselessly through the narrow streets. Just one more unwanted thing trying to install itself.

The first time I encountered him, I was out at night searching for someone I considered a friend—a creature I called the Newb, who was just spilling over the line from puppy to adult dog, as friendly as he was emaciated. I was ready for him, with a ten-rupee pack of Marie biscuits stuffed in the back pocket of my pants. It wasn't the most nutritious meal, but between the biscuits and the meaty table scraps I sneaked out of the house whenever possible, it would be enough, I told myself; or at least, it was the best I could do for him. I tried to believe that was true, but most of the time I knew the Newb was just one more responsibility I was failing at.

I was in the right place—The Newb had made himself a sort of nest at the end of a line of small restaurants, and he usually stayed close to it—but tonight he was nowhere to be seen. In his place was a larger, even more miserable-looking thing.

The word that sprang unbidden to mind (though it wasn't a very nice one) was *cur*. He was in dire shape. When the Newb had first turned up, he, too, had looked deathly ill; but while he was still tiny and knock-kneed, he was clearly gaining weight and getting taller. This thing, this *cur*, was even worse off than the Newb had been—not just emaciated but diseased, his discolored skin almost hairless and scabbed with mange. Yet there was an unnatural sort of vitality to him—his teeth yellow, but sharp and even; his eyes alert despite the gobs of god-knows-what dripping from them. His threadbare tail wagged ferociously. He seemed pleased to see me.

I felt a twinge of pity at his ruined skin, but I had other work to do that night. The Newb had been rallying lately from the frail state he'd arrived in, but still, I didn't want to take any chances. The streets are dog-eat-dog for even the toughest, and the Newb would need more than just his fighting spirit to make it. I wanted to throw in what I could, however inadequate or shitty, to up his odds of making it to adulthood and permanent residence among the dog gangs of the neighbourhood. A newcomer was at best a competitor, at worst a threat, to the Newb's tentative niche here. As far as I knew the Cur had only just turned up, and already he'd usurped the nest of newspaper and rags that the Newb had resourcefully put together.

So I ignored the Cur, peering instead down the narrow alley. Maybe the Newb was lying low just out of sight.

"Newb," I cooed, "come out come out."

The Cur met my eyes and yawned in that way dogs sometimes do when they're trying to telegraph the possibility of friendship. There was a flash of the dog he might have been in another life—a certain brightness despite the state he was in. I told myself I wasn't interested. I didn't wish him ill—it's just that I was here for the Newb, so much younger and less well-versed in survival. I walked past the Cur, deeper into the alley and its wall of ambient noise: voices and TV themes wafting from each of the cramped apartments, a chicken clucking somewhere in the darkness, and the gentle, enduring drone of crickets. There was another sound as well, rasping, repetitive, and arrhythmic. I turned back and saw that it was the Cur, furiously scratching at whichever area of his mangy skin irritated him the most from moment to moment. I felt more than just a twinge of pity then, but still, The Cur was not who I'd come out to look for.

I called for the Newb once, twice, and again and again. The sixth or seventh or ninth time was the charm. He emerged, nose first, from under a crumpled tarp I hadn't noticed. He bounded over in his usual ecstatic way and I dropped to a squat with my arms out, a scene so cutesy it could have been in a Disney movie. Before the Newb could launch himself at me, though, a flash of sound and movement whipped across his path.

It was the Cur, scrambling to an awkward halt between the Newb and me, sending the puppy scrambling back and whining in submission. No big deal. The Cur must have been hungry, and the pack of Marie biscuits might have been enough for two. But then he turned to the Newb and growled, lips curled threateningly away from his teeth, and I had to step in.

"Oi, play nice!"

The Newb had already run off. It was probably the smartest thing for him to do, and while I was disappointed, it was good to know that the little guy had his wits about him.

"Oh, alright. Take your biscuits and go."

I tossed the Cur a couple of biscuits, and he sniffed at them cautiously before lifting his head and flashing me the same snarly face he'd trained on the Newb. He dipped his head again, rooted with his nose to gather the biscuits into a crumbly heap, scooped them into his mouth, and disappeared out the entrance of the alleyway.

"Bon appetit," I called after him.

Next time, I told myself, I'll bring more food. There was an established group of strays that more or less owned the neighbourhood, but other dogs also passed through on occasion, and I suspected I had not seen the last of the Cur. And if the Cur was gone the next time I came back, that would just mean I had extra for the Newb.

Something stirred a few feet away. The Newb, having figured out that the threat had passed, came bounding back out and practically into my lap. Together we carried out what had become our every-couple-of-nights routine, the tiny dog scarfing down what I'd brought while I watched over and petted him. Petting a dog while he ate wasn't a great idea, but I badly wanted us to bond beyond the usual code between dog and human. Flouting this rule of etiquette was worth it if it meant he'd trust me more than most street dogs trust humans. Also, I didn't actually care very much if he bit me.

At that point in my life, aside from the Newb, I didn't care very much about anything at all.

-2-

This largish-house, in a village-suburb at the edge of Chennai, was where my parents had moved after I left home for college. They'd saved up to buy it, and it suited them well, even though the neighbourhood was an odd mix of construction sites, ramshackle apartments, gated communities with high-end aspirations, and small businesses perpetually on the verge of collapse. Incongruent as its various parts felt, this kind of hybrid neighbourhood wasn't unusual on the outskirts of the city. I had never planned to live here myself, but at that point I'd recently been shunted, unwillingly, out of a life I'd started to build elsewhere.

I'd grown up not far from here, in a different nondescript village-suburb of the city, and I'd always wanted out. I had no specific or special reasons why. There were other people who felt stifled by the same things I did: almost every decision anyone made seemed judged and surveilled, any deviation from "our culture" punished. But I guess the others adapted better, or else they adjusted—making workarounds and concessions like hiding who they were dating, concealing things they were really passionate about. I'd tried "adjusting" and it had only frustrated me further.

As I grew up, I did my best to inch further and further away, first from school to college in another state, and then to another college all the way off in the US. I was twenty-two and still abroad when I realised that I wanted, for the first time in my life, to stay instead of leave, that perhaps I'd finally gotten far enough from where I'd begun. There were problems, of course—I'd grown up listening to pop-punk about how the American Dream was a lie, and I'd come to gradually understand the truth of that on the ground—but still I badly wanted to stay. I didn't know how I was going to pull it off, but I was making friends, getting paid to work on things I cared about, even making my parents kind of proud. I dated a guy I felt so-so about and told myself that was part of the deal, that love was work and sometimes work was tedious, that that was the compromise you had to make when everything else was going way too well. Everyone around us seemed to think we were adorable, and how could everyone be wrong?

When my visa ran out about a year into the relationship and no employer would sponsor me to stay, I married him, buying time for us to try to love each other, and borrowing more time for me to try and put down roots that would not fail.

Of course there was a price to pay for this experiment, these attempts to manufacture love and real partnership. Something shifted for him not long after the wedding, warping an unremarkable, even boring relationship into a shadowy and terrifying thing: he would fly into unpredictable rages, accuse me of using him, threaten to pull the green card application that was contingent on our marriage. There were endless scenes of crying and begging, a series of degradations I allowed because there was no other way to keep my life from crumbling. He took what he wanted; by then I was out of legal options to stay, out of ways to say no, unable to shut my legs or my mouth and spit him the fuck out, no matter how much I wanted to be free of it all.

In a way, I did end up free of it all. He made good on his threats, forcing me into what I later learned was called self-deportation. People—friends, colleagues, even my landlady, who had a rolodex of lawyers—did what they could to help, but sometimes an ending is an ending is an ending.

On the flight back to India, I got up several times to stagger to the bathroom and vomit, muscles rippling in reverse until finally I was only spitting up clear fluid with the faintest tinge of blood. Once I'd thrown up for what turned out to be the last time, I scrambled over a sleeping co-passenger and back into my tiny seat, falling asleep almost at once. I dreamed the same thing I'd thought about often since the first time he'd forced himself where I did not want him: of slitting open this body he'd touched, rending part from bloody part, recombining them into something hungry and monstrous, becoming something startling and different and new.

-3-

If only I could figure out how to begin. Since coming back to Tamil Nadu I'd lucked into legal help and a possible way to return, but once the first round of forms was filed there was nothing to do but wait. Someone more resourceful might have found a way to turn this in-between time into productivity (whatever that meant), but I was exhausted, and I hated myself for it. All the reasons I'd wanted to leave in the first place felt starker now. I wanted my old life back—late nights at shows or dive bars or someone-or-the-other's apartment or wherever I wanted to be; the excitement of being paid, no matter how inadequately, to work on things that felt worth the effort; the knowledge that no matter how I dressed or acted, hardly anyone would be bothered enough to give me a hard time. I was too drained to imagine any of those things happening for me again.

I spent the mornings in fitful sleep that was as difficult to shake off as it was to enter in the first place, waking up often and scrolling through page after uninspiring page on job sites until I fell asleep again. I spent the afternoons staring at my computer, endlessly refreshing the same .gov website—the one that might get me the hell out of here—hoping to see something change, knowing that nothing would have. Not just yet.

Most evenings I'd take a walk down to the grocery store, stopping to buy cigarettes and greet the neighbourhood dog gang as I went. I had named them all, and knew each of them to some degree. There was Gambhiran, graying, dappled, and stoic, who presided over the front area of A1 Chinese and Biryani. Two storefronts down, Foxie and Jackie Russell, a cheery bonded pair I thought of as the First Dog Couple of the neighbourhood, made their home at a small complex that included an Aavin milk booth and an Elite Super Mart. Paneer, Pibble, and an ancient, long-limbed, one-eyed presence I called Telescope lived together in the empty plot by Oasis Tea Shoppee.

Foxie and Jackie often followed me on my way back home, delighted to see me even when I had no snacks for them. It took the edge off a bit, being trailed by this happy pair; each time a truck or other large vehicle rumbled past, forcing me to a halt, they'd leap at me for head scratches. This pair were all that mattered in the moment; I found it easy to ignore the dubious looks of passers-by, their insistence on warning me that street dogs were vicious and would bite. The joke was on them—I didn't care what happened to me as long as I could bask in their affection. It was all that meant anything to me at the time.

The Newb appeared on one of these grocery runs, a tiny starved thing shivering behind a pile of old cardboard, and I fell for him immediately. It wasn't as though I had that much control over his future—my parents lived in terror of zoonotic diseases and rabies, and would never have allowed me to foster him in their house—but he was hungry and vulnerable and more life-affirming than anything else around me at the time, and I felt instantly responsible for him. With his pink nose, his short white coat, and jaunty gait (despite his bum leg), he was also too adorable to resist. I had a theory he might have been half Rajapalayam, the result of an illicit house dog/street dog coupling, likely tossed out of a car by people who realised he had no market value. He seemed smart, laying low and keeping out of trouble with the neighbourhood dog gangs, who generally did not welcome newcomers. I hoped that in time they'd come to view him as one of their own, and that I might be able to play some part in making that happen.

Was there room for one more in this little ecosystem, already adjusting to the Newb's arrival? I wasn't so sure, but the Cur, as it turned out, had his ways.

-4-

Each day the sunlit hours went by in a haze of dust and chores and power cuts. Nighttime, no matter how clammy and oppressive, was all mine. I would shower and then lie in bed, dwelling on the idea of dismembering and Frankensteining myself into something bloody and different, until I finally drifted into sleep. I'd usually find myself awake again a few hours later, twitching into consciousness in the dark humid throat of the night.

After a week or two of this I gave up on trying to get back to sleep. Instead, I'd rise from my bed without turning on the lights and make for the door to the terrace, reaching out and curling my hand around my box of cigarettes along the way. The house was taller than every other building around us—despite the trees in the front and back yards, you could see almost the entire neighbourhood if you stood at just the right place on the terrace.

The northern end of the terrace afforded a view of the ramshackle complex opposite us, a two-storeyed building that housed a couple of businesses (Paradise Motors, Sri Jayam Paper Mart, and the memorably named Anarky Food Services); countless rats that appeared sporadically, day and night; and, on particularly hot days, Foxie and Jackie Russell wedged underneath the dust-furred corpse of an ancient car that seemed to have melted into the concrete and dirt in front of Paradise Motors. The southern end of the terrace looked out on a kind of meagre swampland, a small empty plot filled with shallow, weed-choked water and mud. Beyond the swamp lay the village "lake", a waterbody which, in a less arid region, would have been too puny to deserve that name. Other houses and small apartment complexes sat to the east and west, full of neighbors I had hardly seen and wouldn't recognize if I ran into them.

Most nights I'd head to the northern end of the terrace and climb on top of the cement storage nook by the edge of the railing. It was sturdy enough that I could sit on it or even stand up without my fear of heights kicking in. From this perch I could peer out at the road and the Anarky/Paradise/Sri Jayam building, which housed a particular set of nocturnal creatures: an indeterminate number of white cats, the occasional fruit bat weaving through the air to the trees in our garden, and several members of the neighbourhood dog gang, who'd make their way up the street from the restaurants and cafes after sundown to frolic or fight or carry out other dog business under the sickly yellow of the streetlights. There I'd stay, looking out on my friends like a gargoyle, until tiredness overtook me and forced me back to bed.

Sometimes I'd wake feeling unusually rested and find the soles of my feet muddy, mysterious smears of dust or dirt on my pajamas, a smattering of dry leaves and twigs in the snarls of my hair. As a child, I'd sleepwalked occasionally. Nothing worse had ever come of it than scaring the hell out of an unaware cousin of mine during a sleepover. Now that every waking action felt like it cost most everything I had, it was nice to know that there was still some kind of energy animating me, pushing me forward to seek something out, even if I had no idea what that was.

-5-

Most nights it was Foxie and Jackie Russell who would come bounding down the potholed road, but sometimes Telescope would follow them as well, silent but staying close enough to signal that he was part of the team. Occasionally other dogs would drift in from further east, a more aggressive bunch that Foxie and Jackie tried to fend off as best they could. One night I spotted the Newb out on patrol with Foxie and Jackie. He seemed to have gotten himself a job, or at least friends, or allies; and I couldn't help feeling proud even though it wasn't my doing. His sweetness and intelligence were his own, and I was not the only person looking out for him. Several of the workers on the little restaurant row fed him. One, in particular, an older man from the North who I knew only as Bhaiya, had taken to him.

As his fortunes changed, the Newb moved out of his rag-and-newspaper nest in the alleyway; on my walks to the grocery store and back, I saw that he now spent his time in front of Star Royal Biryani, where Bhaiya worked. Bhaiya and I slowly went from exchanging nods to holding conversations about the Newb, who he'd named Chotu. We spoke in a pidgin that bridged the gap between his lack of Tamil, my terrible Hindi, and the sliver of English we both shared. We never spoke about anything else but the dog, but even this interaction carried a sort of warmth, briefly thawing whatever had frozen over inside me. The Newb seemed delighted to have not just one but two surrogate parents. He would perform wild dances around Bhaiya and me when we were together, leaving patterns of shallow bruises on our limbs with his eager, grabby paws.

Usko ghar leke jao na, beti, Bhaiya would say to me sometimes, smiling down at the Newb/Chotu. Take him home with you.

I'd demur each time, my heart breaking a little. As cute as he was, it was a non-starter with my parents. I was grateful for how well the Newb was doing—for the fact that he was being taken care of, even if I was not his primary protector. He seemed like he had a good chance of making it. He had a steady supply of food, at least two humans who loved him, alliances of sorts with his fellow dogs, and a storefront to call his own. Some days I felt like he already *had* made it, that his happyishly-ever-after as a community dog in this place with little community had begun. Stupid as this idea was, it made me feel better about the stasis of my own life—the glacial, grudging job-hunting process, my stalled plans to leave the country, the fact that I was supposedly an adult but lived like a poltergeist shuffling listlessly around in my parents' house. Beneath all this was the series of degradations that had ended me back here in the first place. I told myself I would deal with all that later—once my life changed, I would unpack all this baggage, confront whatever the hell had metastasized inside me. For now, I would bide my time.

-6-

I'd assumed the Cur was a passing visitor, until one night I saw him again, an apparition at the mouth of the Newb's old alleyway. I didn't recognize him at first. I had no idea how it had happened, but his miserable, scabbed coat of mange was gone, replaced by thick, long hair: black, white, and tan in a fetching merle pattern all over, and two rakish patches of red over his rheumy eyes. He was staring right at me, his tail sweeping back and forth in the warm evening air.

"Cur?" I said. "Is that you, buddy?"

He did not get up, but let me approach. When I got within a foot of him, he lifted his head and shot me a grin, and I couldn't help but reach forward to see if he'd let me pet him. I bent and then recoiled. Up close it was clear that even though his mange was gone, he wasn't cured. Those old scabs and crusty patches seemed to have been transfigured, instead, into something else: a gray-and-red galaxy of ticks all over his body. I'd never seen anything like it—clumps of adults with pale, engorged bodies full of blood, and dozens of younger ones crowding around each of the adults, their bodies still tiny and unstretched enough to retain their red color. Or perhaps they were two different species altogether, the Cur's body an unholy menagerie of bloodsuckers. What had looked like cute dots of red fur on his brow were actually masses of the smaller ticks, hanging in clusters above his rheumy eyes.

Beti, usko mat choona. Bahut saare keede hai usme.

I started. Bhaiya and the Newb stood a few feet away in the shadows between the alley and Star Royal Biryani. Bhaiya was right—even if the Cur wanted to be petted, touching his teeming colony of parasites seemed like a bad idea. The Newb came bounding at me then, and by the time I picked myself back up after he knocked me over, the mouth of the alley was empty. Where had the Cur gone?

That was, apparently, just how he did. Bhaiya, who lived in the same run-down building that housed Star Royal Biryani and spent more time around any of the dogs than I did, filled me in. He was well aware of the Cur, though he had not given him a name. The creature had taken up residence in the alleyway, growling at Bhaiya each time he headed down that way to dump trash from the biryani shop into the giant municipal garbage bin. He was, said Bhaiya, an *ajeeb sa chokra*—a weird little guy. He seemed not to eat or socialize. His only interaction with the world was the occasional growl or whine directed at Bhaiya when he walked by.

Voh shayad bimaar hai.

Bhaiya voiced what I was thinking. The Cur probably was sick. None of these dogs were truly healthy, but he was in a league of unwellness all his own.

Bhaiya went on, telling me how he had been trying to keep Chotu away from the Cur, not wanting him to catch whatever the Cur was harbouring. Thankfully, it had been an easy task, despite the Newb's impulse to befriend any nearby dog or human, since the Cur seemed to have little to no interest in other living creatures. Still, he was probably a health hazard in general. Could anything be done about him, Bhaiya wondered? Would I know, perhaps, of an animal rescue that might take him?

We stood in silence for a while, the question hanging between us. I thought of footage I'd seen from "rescues" that turned out to be houses of horror, stories I'd heard of neglect and systemic failures in the municipal shelter. If the Cur were to leave, even if it were to protect the Newb, the right thing to do would still be to check on him, to make sure he was actually being taken care of. That would be my responsibility. Bhaiya had done enough, taking more time and energy than most people would, despite his age and the meagre conditions of his own life.

How did I feel about the Cur? I wasn't sure. It would be nice if he were treated for whatever the hell ailed him, but I had my favorite and so did Bhaiya: it was Chotu/the Newb that we loved and wanted to protect. It wasn't noble and I knew it. I told myself it was because the Newb had been my responsibility first, but it was really the Newb's cuteness, his silliness and abandon and affection, that made him the obvious choice between the two when it came to who we thought of as our own. I wished I knew how to talk to Bhaiya about any of this, but even if I had found the words in English, I probably couldn't have managed to tell him in Hindi.

With the Cur gone for now, Chotu/the Newb did wild puppy pirouettes in the alleyway. We watched him for a few moments before parting. I'll think about it, I told Bhaiya before continuing my walk to the store, I'll see what I can do. There must be someone I can call. Perhaps they could get Chotu fixed up as well, de-worm him and give him his shots.

On my way back from the grocery store I fed all the regulars—Foxie and Jackie Russell first, as usual—ending up empty-handed by the time I reached the alleyway. The Newb was nowhere to be seen. I had a feeling that Bhaiya had semi-adopted him and was probably sneaking him into his quarters at night.

But someone else was waiting for me.

"Hey buddy," I said.

I dug around in my shopping bag, trying to remember if I'd picked up an extra packet of Bony Munch. The Cur watched patiently as I rummaged, shifting occasionally so he could scratch himself and his many vampiric hangers-on. My fingers eventually closed on a crumbling scrap of dog treat. It wasn't much, but I tossed it towards him anyway.

The Cur did not move, watching the morsel of bootleg dog food sail through the air and hit the ground beside him. I made some ridiculous coaxing noises, pointing and wiggling my fingers at the scrap of Bony Munch. The Cur watched me with the same placid gaze. After a few minutes of this futile performance, I accepted that Bhaiya must have been right about never seeing the Cur eat. I told myself it was none of my business why he refused to eat in the presence of humans or other dogs; my business was only to provide him with food. I turned and began to walk away, waiting until I was a safe distance from the alley to turn my head slightly and see if he was now eating my offering.

Instead I saw his jagged-edged shadow making its way from the alley, backlit by a passing car as it crawled over the potholes and fissures of the unmaintained road. I waited for him to get close, though I wasn't sure what to expect. I would pet almost anything that wanted me to pet it, but I drew the line at a creature infested with ticks. I also did not know what the Cur wanted. I stayed there, hoping that I would find out.

He reached within a foot of me and then plunked down, sighing. I called him the name I used for him in my head, Cur, and he raised his head in what seemed like recognition. Still, he did not move. We stayed there for a while in silence. Then I said some kind of goodbye before walking the rest of the way home. The front gate of my parents' compound was close enough that I knew he could still see me. Unlike almost every other dog I knew in the village, he made no attempt to come running over and slip through the open gate, into the front yard. I closed the gate slowly, then made my way to the house.

I paused again before raising my key to the front door, turning back to see if anything had changed. The Cur was in front of the gate now—he must have made a sudden dash from the spot where he'd flopped down sighing just moments earlier. He was now hunched over in a squat, his butt propped against the metal grille of the gate. What a weirdo. I left him to his business, jangling the key in the lock until the right things finally clanked into place, allowing me to disappear again into the house.

-7-

I woke that night on the terrace, sitting cross-legged on my perch by the railing. Something was banging and rattling on the road far below me, the noise of metal colliding with another hard object or surface. It would have been easy enough to sneak quietly back inside the house and into my bed, to lie there with my unease, letting whatever was underway keep happening. But I stayed where I was.

The sound shifted, the rattling giving over to a chorus of howls. This was not the high-pitched staccato shrieking of a bloody internecine dog fight, the kind of thing that erupted by the village lake every couple of nights. This nocturne had more shape, a discernible rise and fall despite the range of voices calling out. There was a suggestion of something more complex than mere aggression, deference, or pain. I straightened up to see what the hell was going on.

It was no surprise to see the Cur right in the eye of things. Around him in a loose semicircle stood all the neighbourhood dogs I knew and some I didn't, heads thrown back and throats bared to the cloudy sky. There was the Newb, too, standing between Foxie and Jackie as if he belonged. I felt a burst of pride that disappeared as quickly as it came. The Cur was the only dog not howling. He cowered, turning his head slowly and looking from face to open-mouthed face of the surrounding pack. Even from a distance I could see that he was shaking with fear. He might not have been the most likable dog around, but I still didn't want to see him maimed, or worse.

I leaned over the railing and yelled the names of the dogs I recognized, each shout getting lost in the din below. None of the animals reacted to me; their raucous song continued, unbroken. By now the Cur had flattened himself to the ground, head laid down against the concrete and dust. It didn't seem to make a difference. The other dogs neither advanced nor fell back; they just stayed in their places and kept up their baying. The Cur rolled over, his belly bared to the pack.

Nothing I knew about dogs—or about these dogs in particular—could help me decipher what I was seeing. It was beyond my understanding, or perhaps simply not meant for me to understand. What could I do but stand there and witness it? A warm breeze blew, plastering a film of dust and several strands of my sweaty hair to my cheek.

Something exploded then, a new burst of noise and sparks showering from the top of an electricity pole. The dogs scattered, their voices trailing off as they disappeared in the many directions from which they had come.

The transformer explosion had apparently taken the village's power supply with it. It seemed like time for me to leave as well. The ceremony—the stand-off, the whatever-it-was—appeared to have concluded.

Before I went back inside, I leaned over the railing once again and squinted into the dark. The Cur was still lying there, pale belly turned up to the sky and its cover of grimy-looking clouds. He was perfectly still, as though the ritual or performance had frozen him in place, but he seemed unscathed—at least, no more scathed than usual.

I turned around and went back into the house, where the power was still out. I took off all my clothes and lay down in the hot, damp maw of my room, hoping to fall asleep. Tomorrow, I promised myself, I would check on the Cur. Tomorrow I would try to figure out what I had just witnessed.

-8-

I started following some local animal rescue organizations online. They seemed to have their hands full with an endless line of battered creatures, but I figured they might be able to give me some leads on what I could do for the Cur. What had happened the previous night was no clearer to me, but I didn't want to take the chance that what I'd witnessed had been an excommunication, that he'd worn out the welcome he barely had.

I stayed in bed as I looked up numbers and drafted DMs. Someone picked up barely two rings after I made the first phone call, a girl who sounded around my age. I tried not to open with apologies—*sorry I live so far away and am about to ask if you might do a pick-up because I can't bring this tick-ridden dog to you in my parents' car, sorry I don't know how to deal with this on my own even though I am supposedly an adult, sorry I'm bothering you with this instead of giving you the donations or time your animals clearly need, sorry.* I tried to tell her about the Cur.

"His name is the Cur," I started saying, but it felt wrong calling him that outside my own head, where it wasn't apparent that my feelings about him were more complex than that name might imply.

A burst of static chewed up my words, giving me a chance to do it over.

"Sorry?" said the girl on the other end. "Connection dropped for a moment."

"Oh. Yes, sorry. So yeah, his name is Curd Rice, but he also answers to Buddy. Well, he doesn't really answer to anything, but that's what I call him..."

Where was all this babbling coming from? Why couldn't I speak in clear sentences? What use would any of this be to this girl listening patiently as I tried to explain what the Cur's deal was, what I thought he might need?

The girl cut in gently.

"I'm so sorry, Ma'am," she said, sounding genuinely chagrined. "The location you mentioned, it's out of our range for pickups. Could you bring him in?"

A flash of the constellation of ticks that I'd come to think of as part of the Cur's being. Of the blend of mistrust and fear that I'd seen almost every time I looked in his eyes. Of his eyes themselves, dripping with gobs of something thick and pale.

I said something quick and ashamed, apologizing again before I hung up. I left my phone in my room and walked outside, slipping by my parents, who would no doubt want to know where I was headed and what for. I did not want to explain.

I got to the gate, where the next thing to throw me off lay in wait. The grille that made up the gate's lower half was busted, its pattern of curlicues jagged and broken as though the metal had suddenly, spontaneously crumbled... or been ripped off. I recalled the clattering and banging that had woken me up the night before. The metal must have rusted enough under its coat of paint to break when whatever-it-was was bumping up against it. I decided against touching the gate at all and stayed inside the yard. If something else was going to fall apart, I wanted no part of it.

I still needed a breath of different air, though. I needed to be out there in the heat until it seared the ugly feeling out of my chest. There were few vehicles on the road this early, and I had a clear view of the Anarky/Paradise building opposite the house. There the Cur was, of course, in exactly the same place he'd been the night before—but sitting up this time, goop-ringed eyes trained right on my own.

Ah, fuck. I went back indoors, managing to evade my parents once again, and returned with a package of Bony Munch. As I opened the gate carefully I noticed a cairn of pebble-shaped poop right outside. I couldn't help but think of it as some kind of marking, an "I was here" or some other message left for whoever knew how to read it. I looked at the Cur and he looked blankly back from under his tiara of ticks, holding my gaze until I reached his side of the street, ripped open the thick plastic wrapping of the Bony Munch, and scattered the bumpy, unnaturally yellow sticks near him.

The Cur growled, lips pulled back in the classic pose I'd seen in rabies PSAs and stock photos of canine aggression. I fell back promptly. He leaned forward and sniffed at the sticks for a moment before scarfing up as many of them as he could fit in his mouth. I felt something like satisfaction as he trotted off, still chewing, dipping into the trash-choked gutter that snaked between the road and the frontage of the Anarky/

Paradise building. Just to make the feeling last, I stepped cautiously closer, hoping to catch a glimpse of him eating.

But he wasn't eating. He dropped the snacks amongst the dirt and garbage that filled the gutter, then dove in and began to dig. He popped back up with something else in his mouth, leaping out of the gutter surprisingly nimbly before walking over to me and sitting down with a huff. He didn't growl when I looked at him this time, but he didn't return my gaze either. He just sat there with his find—something metallic and jagged, perhaps some kind of gear from Paradise Motors—and, after a little while, began to chew.

"Buddy," I said. "You shouldn't be eating that. You *can't* eat that."

But he could. I stared as his jaws worked, clamping down with unnatural force as he split the metal easily, pausing occasionally to slurp down the mush he'd chewed it into. I dropped into a squat so I could watch more closely. This close up, I could see the ticks all over him, despite the thickness of his fur, a sick constellation undulating across his skin. The Cur just kept on chewing and swallowing. When he was done, he craned his neck and let out a small cough. I caught a glimpse of something bright and metallic flashing in the shadows behind his teeth.

All this while, workers came in and out of Anarky/Paradise. By now they were used to seeing me hanging out with some dog or several, and nobody looked twice at the Cur and me.

He coughed once more, louder this time, and spat. A wad of something chewed-up hit the dirt. It was orange and glowing as though pulled from a fire.

"Buddy," I murmured.

The Cur licked his lips and continued to ignore me.

"Cur? Curd Rice?"

Motorbikes and cars were starting to crowd the street. More workers arrived. The shutters of Anarky Food Services and Paradise Motors creaked and rattled their way up behind the Cur and me. Across the street, the front door of my parents' house swung open slowly. One of them must have woken up, heading outside to collect the newspaper as they did every morning. I stood up and darted through a sudden gap in the traffic, making it through the gate and shutting it behind me.

"Morning, Amma," I called. "You don't have to come out. I was just getting some air. I'll bring the newspaper in."

She yelled something back that I couldn't make out, and the door shut again. I picked the newspaper up off the ground and turned around. The Cur was sitting there still. A couple of the Anarky workers walked past him to dump something in the thorn bushes nearby. None of them seemed to notice him or the little chunk of hot metal he'd spat up, still glowing brightly enough to be visible despite the sunlight.

-9-

I am woken by a sensation in my feet and at the base of my spine, something hard and unforgiving protesting against my weight. I feel sweat pooling in the folds of my belly, in the crevices behind my knees, dripping slowly down my forehead. I am sitting hunched over on the same rough slab of concrete that the Cur occupied earlier, chewing his metallic cud before coughing it up, red-hot. I am not alone. The Cur is beside me, closer than I've ever gotten to him during any sane hour. I do not know how I got here.

"Cur," I say.

He ignores me, which is the only part of this moment that feels normal. I want to stand up but I can tell I don't have the energy yet. As I gather myself, I hear the Cur move. I watch him disappear into the gutter, listen as he digs furiously among the trash. He returns and sits next to me, what looks like a broken-off part of a power tool in his mouth.

"Hey, buddy."

I scooch closer to him as he begins to chew, and he lets me. I talk to him, spilling all the troubles that have been roiling in my gut, saying things I have never said out loud, things I have tried to text to friends but then hastily deleted, because admitting how precarious I feel might shatter what little stability I have left, might raise alarms and cause them to worry, might then require me to reassure them that I'll be alright, even if I'm not sure that I will be, just so they leave me alone.

The Cur seems not to care. I think that is why I can say these things in front of him. I am no concern of his.

He keeps chewing, not looking at me. I raise my arm and extend it towards him. He notices it and slides me a meme-worthy side-eye, the metal whatsit half-hanging out of his mouth at a jaunty angle.

"May I?"

I expect a growl or at least a grimace, the same curled-back lips and exposed teeth he has flashed at me before. But he does nothing—just accepts the warmth of my palm against the back of his neck, allowing me to carefully rake my fingers through his long, thick fur. He leans into my palm, shutting his eyes as I stroke his head and neck. I feel scabs and bumps under my fingertips, the distended bodies of ticks round and full against my skin. The sensation sends goosebumps and a vague disgust blossoming through me. But I stay there, quiet now and feeling different, lighter in a way I cannot yet process.

-10-

It kept happening. Some mornings I woke up on the floor, curled and fetal. Some nights must have been more chaotic than others; more than once I found myself standing outside the locked gate with no idea how I had gotten out there, ultimately deciding that slapstick was the only way back in—clambering awkwardly over the gate, adding rust and paint chips to the mess of stains and smudges on my pajamas before thudding into the yard. I took to washing my pajamas by hand, tendrils of red and brown blossoming among the suds as I shoved the wadded-up fabric into a bucket of soapy water.

Somehow I managed all this without my parents being the wiser. Occasionally I'd wake up in the early morning standing in the yard; but it was easy to pretend that I'd come out to do dutiful daughterly morning things like pick up the newspaper and unlock the gate. To my parents, I just seemed to be waking up earlier, and at breakfast they liked to talk about what a good development that was, how I must be making *progress*. I'd smile and nod over toast or idlis or whatever was on the table, barely eating as I sifted through what remained in my mind of the night before. I seemed to have no trouble remembering actually being out there, pajama-covered butt perched awkwardly on what I'd come to think of as The Cur's throne, coughing up every feeling I suppressed during the daytime into his tattered ears while he chewed on the latest piece of castoff metal he'd found. The memory gave me a sort of energy, and I found it easier to put one foot in front of the other from one day to the next, still organizing papers and thinking about jobs and returning again, again, again to the USCIS website. I felt something like hope now each time I logged in, a real sense that this could be the day some news, perhaps even good news, might arrive.

-11-

One of those mornings I was woken by a thud, followed by a sound so unearthly I couldn't begin to guess what it was. It snapped me right out of bed and down the stairs. When I stepped outside, the gate was already unlocked, though nobody else was up yet—it seemed I was now sleepwalking through my early morning duties like an automaton, not needing to be truly awake. There were few vehicles on the road and the noise, a weird yowling, was already dying down. By now I was sure that someone or something was hurt, and judging by the weakening of the cries, getting worse by the moment.

I ran up the road, clumsy in my too-large chappals.

As I neared the row of small restaurants, I saw it—a lump in the road, heaving slowly and moaning. *Fuck.* Up ahead restaurants were starting to open, shutters groaning as they rolled up, releasing the sounds and smells of breakfast being cooked. People walked on the narrow edge of the road, their gazes fixed determinedly ahead. I stepped into the road, feeling each pothole and sharp chunk of rubble through the soles of my chappals.

It was Telescope. His mouth was open and he was trying his hardest to suck in the dusty air. His lower half was mangled; a mess of bone, blood, and tissue was smeared in a trail from the place where some vehicle must have hit him. He had dragged himself here, just a foot or two shy of the roadside and its relative safety.

I tasted tears and snot, panic blurring my vision. Was it too late for him? Could I try to get him off the road myself, or would that hurt him worse? I looked uselessly into his one good eye and he held my gaze. A scooter and then a car whizzed by, both of them too close for comfort, and honking at me. But I could not move. I heard myself mumbling his name.

A shout rang out over the buzzing in my head.

Beti! Kya hua?

Bhaiya and the Newb stood at the mouth of the alley, the old man holding an empty pail and the Newb taking in what he saw before starting to howl in anguish. Telescope's breathing picked up again, a low moan making its way impossibly out of his ruined body. My paltry Hindi would not come, and I waved my arms stupidly at Telescope as if Bhaiya couldn't already see what was happening.

Bhaiya spoke sharply then, more authoritative than I had ever heard him.

Sadak se hat jao, Beti. Get off the road.

I couldn't move. I wanted everything to come undone, everything back to the first instant I'd felt anything at all in this life. I wanted to be smeared across rough concrete and then erased by tire track after track, my life instead of Telescope's.

Bhaiya called out again.

Chotu ko pakad lo, beti. Nahi to woh bhaagega.

Hearing his voice and the Newb's name snapped me back into my body. I turned to nod at Bhaiya in acknowledgement, and we traded places—Bhaiya moving towards the ragged bed of gore where Telescope lay while I made for the Newb, scooping him into my arms. He nestled against me—shaking and whimpering, but safe from the risk of running out into the road.

Bhaiya stood up from the crouch he'd assumed over Telescope, the look on his face telling me what I already knew. He told me to stay where I was, to hold on to Chotu while he went to get a gunny sack or something to carry Telescope off the road. I nodded, snuggling the Newb closer, trying to calm myself with breath after breath of his puppy-dog smell. Telescope had fallen silent, his ribcage no longer rising or falling. Now it was only a matter of keeping him from more indignity, or at least of convincing ourselves that we were doing all that we could.

Just then something came hurtling up the road towards us. I had never imagined the Cur was capable of moving so fast, or of skidding so deftly to a halt right by Telescope. He dipped his head, practically falling over himself to root enthusiastically in the warm, wet tatters of Telescope's lower body.

"HEY!" I heard myself shout.

The Cur raised his head to look at me, his tail moving in broad, happy wags. His face was crusted with blood and tissue I could not identify. One of the long bones of Telescope's legs was stuffed in his mouth. Then he was gone again just as suddenly as he'd come, a dirty gray blur receding swiftly down the road.

Bhaiya returned shortly afterwards, a makeshift winding sheet in his arms. He must have seen the look on my face.

Kya hua, Beti? Kuch aur hua kya?

I could only shake my head. The words to describe what I'd just seen wouldn't come to me. I had that feeling the Cur inspired so often, that I was witnessing something utterly alien and confounding. Perhaps what I had seen was not for me to tell.

Kuch nahi, Bhaiya. Kuch nahi.

-12-

There is a sensation in my feet and at the base of my spine, something hard and unforgiving protesting against my weight. I feel sweat pooling in the folds of my belly, in the crevices behind my knees, dripping slowly down my forehead. Something soft and warm is in my lap, its breath blowing sporadic and cool against my damp pajamas. My hand is in its fur, and the feeling of something skittering beneath my fingertips snaps me closer to wakefulness.

The Cur lies against me, his head nestled on my thigh. He is breathing gently, half asleep. I am not sure how I keep from starting in shock, or at least from crying out. He turns his gaze to meet mine, one rheumy eye looking up into my own sunken pair. His muzzle is still crusty with blood and other gunk that used to be part of Telescope. I carefully withdraw my hand from the crown of his head and a clump of his hair comes with it.

I am speaking to the Cur. I am asking him for answers that I know will not come. I am pleading with him, trying to strike a bargain: I told you the things I did to myself and the things that were done to me; I told you my stupid secrets; I told you things I tell no one. I told you what it was like to be pinned down and run through by someone who had seemed too boring to ever truly hurt me; I told you about aching to claw myself out of a body and a life that felt ruined—too much of them taken through force and threats ever to be close to whole again; I told you how it felt to realise that there is always something worse waiting in the wings, hungry and patient. Tell me about *you* now. Tell me what was done to you; tell me what you are trying to do in this place, aside from survive; tell me why you are all alone, without a single other dog as your friend or ally.

My pleading summons something. A sound of paws skittering over dust and unevenly tarred road. I turn and see the Newb approaching.

"Hi, baby," I say. I am not certain if he should be here. I don't know how this is supposed to go. I think I'm ready to protect him if the Cur goes on the offensive.

But of course I've misjudged the whole thing. The Cur greets the smaller dog with his usual non-reaction, a deep sigh the only sign of acknowledgement. The Newb pads over and nestles against my right thigh, as if balancing a scale made lopsided by the Cur's head on my left. He wiggles a little and leans forward, sticks out his tongue to lick the crust off the Cur's muzzle. To my surprise, the Cur lets this happen, even heaving another sigh as the smaller dog cleans the gunk off his face. It comes to me that all three of us are hungry, that perhaps there is nothing out of the ordinary here to anyone who understands that and can see things as they really are. Everything the Cur does must be what he needs to do to survive and keep going—outlandish as that looks to someone like me, someone uncomprehending. I think, in my way, I am trying to do the same.

I pet both their heads, tracing slow patterns atop their skulls. Above us the sky is dark pink, the moon round and fuzzy behind a tissue of low-lying clouds. Slowly, the sticky breeze blows the clouds away, but the moon still looks indistinct and blurry at the edges. Then it begins to rain, slow fat drops falling lazily onto us. Smells rise into the air as raindrops splatter, trash and earth and skin and fur all giving up their odors. The three of us smell the same: a hybrid of canine and human and things unnameable and dank. Sitting like this—a dazed, unwashed bootleg Madonna flanked by my grubby companions—I can't remember the last time I felt as connected to anything. Not to a friend, not to a lover, not to my body. Not to whatever it is that people call a self.

-13-

I woke the next morning to hammering rain, a putrid, metallic taste in my mouth and an insistent tickling in my throat. Stumbling out of bed and into the bathroom, I coughed and retched until at last I hawked up what looked like tiny, deflated berries—or maybe grapes—in a pool of bloody phlegm.

Stranger things have happened, I told myself. I'd had sinusitis all my life; I had coughed up mysterious somethings before. It was just like me to forget that I'd absent-mindedly grazed my way through a bowl of grapes the previous night. Things get weird as they move through a body, after all, losing form and identifiability. I ran the faucet and spat again and again until the splatters in the sink went from red to pale brownish pink. Then I brushed my teeth.

When I was done, I sat in bed and reached for my phone and water bottle. As I drank, I looked at my phone and immediately swallowed the wrong way out of shock. There it was on my screen: a flash of hope, an email address that ended with .gov. I tapped the screen and read it, and while its language was tentative and obscure, it seemed that *something* was happening, that my case was moving forward in a queue that, for the first time, seemed finite. At long fucking last, I was the tiniest bit closer to getting out of here.

Who to tell? The answer was obvious to me, more urgent and immediate than anyone I had in any inbox or contact list. But it was raining too hard to comfortably leave the house, sheets of water pouring down so that the morning looked more like dusk. The Cur and the Newb had to be hiding from the weather. Still, I felt compelled to grab the sturdiest umbrella I could find and head outdoors to find them. The previous night was fresh in my mind: dreamlike, beguiling, vivid.

Outside, the street was a shallow gray river. Anarky Foods and Paradise Motors were shuttered, the last few workers wading through filthy rainwater as they left the building. But there the two dogs were, sitting regally on the cement block I'd come to think of as ours. The Cur stared and the Newb wagged his tail.

"You guys!" I yelled. "It's happening! It's finally happening."

The umbrella was little help against the water and wind. I folded it up as best I could without snapping its flimsy ribs, then stood there and grinned idiotically as the rain slapped against me from a hundred different directions.

"You should get out of the rain," I yelled across the street. "I'll come see you after it quiets down."

The Newb responded with barks and a twirly little dance before hopping off the block and wading up the road, as if he'd been waiting for me to give him permission to leave and make for shelter—an awning, a nook, perhaps even a corner of Bhaiya's quarters. The Cur just sat, rheumy eyes trained on mine. Despite the rain there was still a trace of redness on his muzzle, dark chunks visible in his fur even through the rain and across the street.

"Thank you, Buddy," I called before turning around and wading back to the house.

Of course the Cur had not shown any reaction. I wasn't sure why, but telling him the news felt like the right thing to do, and thanking him did, too.

-14-

The rain did not let up for about a week and a half. A stubborn, hacking cough kept me indoors, and various tasks kept me busy: phone calls with friends I'd ghosted but finally felt able to reach out to; endless searches for documents, records, and email threads that USCIS had now requested.

If I was still sleepwalking out onto the road at night, I couldn't tell. I awoke a few times with muddy feet and damp clothes, but there was no way to know whether I'd just gone out onto the terrace or ventured into the muck outside. I slept soundly and remembered almost nothing.

Here is the *almost*: a dream I had repeatedly, though I could not say how many times. It took place in a landscape that felt hermetic and arcane, distinct from both the "real" waking world and the liminal realm I seemed to inhabit while sleepwalking. The dream was peopled—or *dogged*, rather—by characters that made up my day to day: the Cur, the Newb, the rest of our canine neighbors. They were arranged in a semicircle, howling the same weird song they had howled on that night I had watched them gather around the Cur. But I knew I was dreaming because I was both myself and one of them; an inchoate creature positioned both literally and figuratively between the Cur and the others.

In the dream, The Newb stepped forward from the choir as I stepped backwards, as I threw in my lot instinctively with the Cur. I had no thoughts. Powered by everything roiling inside me that I could not name, I dropped to the ground, standing on all fours, pawing the dirt before spreading my jaws to let out the roar that had been building up in my bones. I was not a dog, not a werewolf, just myself. Noise and static, dirt and shadow, crashes and sparks and burning, hemmed in by a girl-shaped barricade of flesh. I was louder than all the dogs calling in unison. Perhaps I was more powerful, too; or perhaps I was too ridiculous to be worth their time. It didn't matter which it was. Their voices dropped and they began to disperse, heads lowered in what could have been either fear or embarrassment at my pageantry.

Only the Newb kept advancing, with steps much slower than he ever would have taken outside of a dream. I held my hands out as I had so many times before, letting him come to me, before scooping him to my chest and cradling him. I felt his heart beating against my breastbone, felt the breath move in and out of his body. I turned around to face the Cur, who was not cowering but standing and staring right at me.

I knew then what needed to be done, and I did it.

It was slow but quiet, the Newb's little body going slack as I chewed, sawing through fur and sinew and exposing his insides. If he tasted of anything, that sensation did not follow me out of the dream; I remember only heat, something intoxicating passing from his ruined tissues to mine.

The Cur and I moved in unison then, him rising on his hind legs as I leaned downwards to let him take the offering daintily from my stained mouth into his. I watched him eat, and when he was done we curled up and lay down together, huddling for warmth. As his breathing slowed and deepened I reached through the thicket of fur on his head, fingertips closing around the taut, fat body of a tick, prying it from his skin and slipping it into my mouth. I felt its tiny legs wriggle as I popped it between my teeth, its warm insides squirting against the roof of my mouth. The Cur sighed and began to snore.

Each time I left this dream I woke to a weight in my belly, a weird taste in my mouth that reminded me of something I couldn't place. I'd force myself out of bed, glug water and brush my teeth to try and wash out the sourness. I'd tell myself it was just the cold teaching itself new tricks inside my body, that the dreams were just a sign that I missed the Cur and the Newb. I decided to wait until the rain let up and then go out and find my two friends, whether in the daylight or in the in-between place where we'd hang out at nighttime.

-15-

When the rain finally stopped, I left the house almost immediately, not bothering to change my flimsy chappals before stomping through the river of runoff that had replaced the dirt road. The Cur was not on his throne in front of Anarky/Paradise, but that was no surprise—even he needed shelter from the rain. The further I went the more choked the road grew, the water barely flowing between heaps of uncollected refuse that spilled over from the roadside. The sun hid behind thick billows of cloud, as it had for weeks, casting a sullen light on everything.

A few of the eateries seemed to be open. I saw the shapes of people moving around inside, smelled a pungent compound of masalas, burning milk, rot, and garbage. The row of yellow lights above the A1 Chinese and Biryani sign was on—flickering, but hanging in there. Jackie Russell was sitting by herself in what had been the Newb's special place, right in front of A1. I had never seen her without Foxie before. As I grew closer she got up and walked off.

"Jackie," I called. "Jackie Russell, it's me!"

She kept walking, trotting away through the dark water.

I felt cold all of a sudden, the excitement that had brought me this far slumping into dread. There were men inside A1, setting up the kitchen and speaking Tamil in low voices, but I did not recognize any of them.

"Hello?" I said. "*Anna*?"

I was shivering and foolishly dressed, sodden in my pajamas and chappals. They turned to me and asked, straight-faced, what was up. I grasped for words. I had never known Bhaiya's name. Was that uncle there, I tried asking, the older one who spoke Hindi? They shook their heads.

Theriyale, ma. Naanga inniku thaan vandhirukko.

Of course they'd only just turned up. I should have guessed as much since I didn't recognize any of them, and I'd known all of Bhaiya's three or four coworkers by sight.

I tried again. Had they seen a small white dog with a pink nose and a slight limp? More head-shakes, some looks of sympathy. Thank you, I mumbled, before wading back home in a guilty rage at myself. I shouldn't have waited this long. I should have come out despite the rain and my cough—so what if I'd gotten sicker? I would have gotten well again eventually. I should have at least gone as far as the roof or the gate to see what I could of the Cur's throne at Anarky/Paradise; leaned out as far as possible for a glimpse at restaurant row; I should have watched for a flash of the Newb's white fur in the small, waterlogged world. Whatever had happened in the time I was housebound felt like my fault, like I'd stumbled into the midst of something that was never mine to meddle with and set something in motion that I didn't understand.

-16-

I am standing on the Cur's concrete throne, more awake than I have been in months. I am surrounded by faces I recognize—Foxie, Jackie Russell, Pibble, Paneer, Gambhiran—and several I do not. The Newb is not among them. I hear the voices of the pack all around me, the rise and fall of their nocturne, the current it carries of something beyond mere aggression, deference, or pain. I want to call out their names, but my body is otherwise occupied. Every muscle in my trunk seems to be twisting, working towards some excruciating, nauseating goal. I retch and cough up bile, then something more substantial that scratches its way up my esophagus and out of my mouth, landing with a *squelch* on the dirt in front of Anarky/Paradise. I don't dare look down.

I scan the faces of the baying crowd again. Most of them don't meet my eyes. Those that do whip their heads back immediately, showing their vibrating throats. I almost wish they'd close in on me, do something to set things right. But they remain where they are, neither advancing or retreating.

Another wave of nausea hits me, another burst of pain making its way from my belly to my chest to my throat. It forces me into a squat, leaving me no choice but to look at what I've already spewed.

Illuminated faintly by moonlight, it is a jumble of nearly-recognizable parts: something curved and pointy, something like a clump of white fur, several somethings that look like tiny, pale pink beans. *Please*, I think, managing to raise my head to look again at the assembly, their eyes a wall of beady lights keeping me corralled. *Please make it stop*, I think, even as I realise that what I want doesn't matter. It's very far from over. Another wave of retroperistalsis begins. As I try to steady myself, a thought rears up as ferociously as the taste of blood and acid filling my mouth, the feeling of something large and sharp tearing its way up through my body, towards my face. *This is a beginning. I am getting exactly what I deserve.*

Ice Cream Boy

JUGAL MODY

PART I

It was a hot summer afternoon. The loudest of vendors and the chattiest of neighbours were asleep. The street was quiet—save for the soft soundscape of the neighbourhood's thousand whirring fans, garnished with the hiss of the chaiwala's stove and his pateli-chamcha clangs. Everyone had sprinkled laxman rekhas of water around them to keep the heat out—street vendors around their carts, people on benches in the parks, people at home around their cots. Aarti seemed to be the only one awake in the entire neighbourhood. The identical twins from across the street, who normally would've been throwing water at each other on their terrace like it was Holi, had been slapped asleep by their mother.

Aarti's mother worked at the bank; she wouldn't be back for a few hours. The fan chopping above Aarti's head creaked ever so slightly with every rotation. Aarti's physics textbook had taught her that this happened because the plane of rotation of the fan was at a small angle with the motor suspended perpendicularly from the ceiling.

Aarti rocked back and forth on the floor. Pages of practice diagrams of the animal cell and the plant cell fluttered in front of her. Her eyes were rolled to the back of her head so as not to glance at the textbook in her hand. She recited the different parts of the cells. "Cytoplasm, nucleoplasm, mitochondrion, Golgi apparatus, ribosome, lysosome, peroxisome, vacuole..."

A metallic shuffle from the front door broke Aarti's concentration. The operator of the key was obviously unaware of the correct angle at which it had to be slid into the lock for it to click open. Aarti's eyes rolled back down. The hair on her arms and legs rose on end. She jumped up. Her knees straightened, like broken sticks unbreaking themselves. Was it a burglar? Aarti's breath froze in her lungs. Then she heard the voice cussing at the door.

She instantly exhaled and smiled. It was her father.

•

Aarti's father was an officer of the National Information and Security Wing. This was something Aarti was not supposed to know. Her parents told her that he worked in financial risk mitigation in London. They maintained this story despite Aarti having caught them in the lie a few times.

Once, when she was alone at home, she had made it a mission to find evidence with which to confront her father. She had found a British passport and a Saudi Arabian passport, both bearing her father's photo, but with different names. She hid them in her school bag to confront her parents when they returned. That night, she made her accusation over dinner: "I have proof." Her father asked her to produce the so-called proof she claimed to have. She washed her hands and opened her school bag to find that the evidence had gone missing.

Aarti had had a raging fit. She screamed at him for stealing the passports from her bag and ran out of the house. She spent a few hours crying on a bench in the neighbourhood park.

A little past midnight, her father, carrying a packed suitcase, joined her on the bench. Looking at the bag, she knew he was going to be gone for one of his long trips. He held her and said, "Ma and I will forgive you for what happened today…"

Before he could say anything else, Aarti started punching him in the chest. "You're a liar! Get lost!" She had never felt as betrayed by anything in her life as she had that day. A few windows opened and neighbours looked out into the park to see who was screaming. Not to cause further commotion, her father quietly got up and left. Aarti's mother let her cry in the park, knowing she would come home when she was done.

Despite this incident, during the Independence Day and Republic Day celebrations at school, Aarti always felt herself swell with pride. During the flag hoisting and the singing of the national anthem, she stood with her chest thrust further than any other kid in school, because she knew her father was putting his life on the line for the country.

•

"How can you forget how to open your own lock?" she asked as she opened the door. "You must be the worst spy in the history of intelligence."

"Not a spy. I am an actuarial officer for a British MNC." Her father dropped his bag and the two of them hugged tightly, without letting go for a couple of minutes.

"I wonder why we're living in this rundown house in nowhere lane then." Aarti wept quietly against her father's shirt. The last time he'd left for "London" in the middle of the night, she hadn't had the chance to hug him.

"I missed you too, you know?" He placed his palm where her plait started. "It's your mother's birthday, you remember that, right? Let's do up the place. I brought decorations."

By the time the rest of the neighbours had woken up from their nap, the father and daughter had done up the house.

In his excitement to spend time with her, he hadn't bothered to wash up or change. When he finally got around to washing his face, they heard the honk of the ice cream truck entering their lane. This was a neighbourhood ritual of sorts. The ice cream truck always passed through their lane to avoid the traffic on the main road. To compensate for the trouble of allowing his large vehicle to pass through their small lane, the driver sold the ice cream at a discount to everyone who lived there. Buying that discount-price ice cream was Aarti and her father's favourite thing to do together whenever he was in town.

She asked him to go and stand in line. "I'll come in five minutes."

Aarti didn't normally bother about her appearance when she stepped out of the house. More often than not, she could be seen parading around in her father's pyjamas, rolled up at the ankles and tied at the waist. She only ever bothered to dress up when she stepped out with her father.

As she had just about managed to slip her ankle into the bunched-up leg of her skinny jeans, she heard the vroom of a speeding engine. People screamed warnings asking someone to watch out for the car. The trumpet tune of the musical electric horn of the ice cream truck sounded off relentlessly. The vrooming got louder. She slid the jeans leg off her ankle, pulled her father's pyjamas back on, and ran to the door... only to see a speeding sedan run straight into her father. He flew a few feet and collapsed next to the ice cream truck. After that his body did not move. The ice cream truck driver dropped the box of ice creams he was pulling out of the back and ran to Aarti's father's unmoving corpse. Aarti wanted to run to him but found herself unable to budge. Her brain screamed at her body to move but it wouldn't listen. The car screeched its tires and sped away.

The onlookers gasped. Children screamed. A crowd gathered around her father. Aarti saw her mother, returning from the bank, enter the lane. She wanted to ask her mother not to go and look, but she couldn't open her mouth; her words couldn't find themselves. The neighbourhood ladies grabbed Aarti's mother and tried to stop her from working her way through the crowd, but it was as if she already knew what had happened. When she reached the centre of the throng, blood drained from her face and a shriek pierced the air.

That was the last day the ice cream truck came through their lane.

During her final exams that year, Aarti drew the diagrams of the plant cell and animal cell perfectly, but she couldn't remember the names of all the cell parts. Her tears blurred some of the ones she did remember. So she received only half the marks for the diagram, and none for the labelling.

Summer vacation went by without much happening. Her mother's birthday decorations, put up by Aarti and her father, stayed on the walls. There were no great changes in Aarti's and her mother's daily routines after her father's death, except that each found the other staring blankly into space a lot more often. The only thing that Aarti heard day and night was the chaiwala's kerosene burner's hiss, the chamcha clanging against the pateli, and the whirring of the neighbourhood's hajaar fans. No other sound or voice made it to her ears.

That year, winter came early and it came hard. The meteorological phenomenon was discussed on news channels across the world. It wasn't just that the sun never made an appearance: it actually snowed. It snowed in places it had never snowed before, including Aarti's neighbourhood.

PART II

It snowed every day for seven years after Aarti's father died. For the first couple of years, people held onto the hope that everything would go back to normal "any day now." People learned how to layer up and shovel snow off their terraces. The municipal corporation fixed makeshift sheets of metal in front of garbage trucks to plough snow off the roads. It was when the damp corpses of trees began falling that people started taking the matter seriously.

Alcohol sales spiked tremendously in those years. The chaiwala in Aarti's lane served his tea with a couple of spoonfuls of name-the-drink in it. The identical twins who lived opposite her house, who had once spent their summer afternoons playing with water, were now busy drinking rum or whiskey stolen from their father's cabinet. Even Aarti's mother took to polishing off a couple of teaspoons of brandy before she went to bed.

Aarti stayed as far away from alcohol as possible. She was glad she didn't have any friends to peer pressure her into drinking. In college, she sat with two girls on the last bench. One of them was constantly playing with her hair—lifting a lock of hair taut to its end and then letting it fall over her face, and then onto the next lock of hair, till she looked like the stereotypical girl ghost from every horror movie. The other girl was always fishing out cosmetics from her bag, arranging them on her desk, counting every item, and then putting them back in.

While everybody else wore layers upon layers, Aarti wore only t-shirts—as though it was a forever summer—and jeans, which she chose over shorts or pyjamas only because her thighs got too cold. It was the same pair of jeans she had tried (and failed) to wear on the day her father died. When her thighs outgrew the jeans, she got the neighbourhood alteration tailor to take every stitch of the jeans apart, add extra fabric, and stitch it all back together. She didn't wash that pair for months. On the day they did finally go to wash, Aarti wore her dad's old boxers, and did not leave the house till the pair of jeans had dried and she could wear them again.

Though Aarti wasn't tempted by alcohol, she did pick up smoking during her college years. She smoked four cigarettes a day. The first was outside the college gate before the first lecture. The second was on the motorised cycle rickshaw (the motor had been added after the snow) on her way back home. The third was after dinner, and the fourth was late at night before she tried to go to sleep. She usually smoked this last cigarette on the same bench in the neighbourhood park where she had once gone to cry.

Aarti smoked because it kept the padhaakus and behenjis away from her (or so she explained it to herself). She didn't have to worry about the other students because her sartorial choices ensured she was invisible to them. She wasn't worried about attention from the boys either. The expression she wore on her face every day kept them away just fine.

One night, after her mother downed a full katori of brandy instead of her usual two spoons, Aarti went to the park for her last cigarette of the day. She wiped the snow off one end of the bench and spread out the dry plastic sheet that she carried with her every night. She sat on it and lit her cigarette.

She was a few drags in when a figure appeared from behind the trees. It looked a lot like the Pillsbury Doughboy, but with rougher edges. It seemed to be covered in a quilt of various colours—most of them pastel except for a red and a dark brown. It trudged towards Aarti, who continued to smoke as if she hadn't noticed it. The figure reached the bench and sat on the other end.

Aarti continued to smoke as she stared blankly at the swing set and the jungle gym. The figure sighed deeply and made some other attention-seeking noises. Aarti did not respond. It then stood up and took a sideways step to the left, moving closer to Aarti, and sat down again. Still, Aarti did not react. Aarti could smell the sweetest vanilla scent she had ever come across. It was mingled with mango and watermelon.

"I'll scream, okay?" she warned the being.

"Ice cream, okay?" said a voice, which sounded like a young man, perhaps in his 20s. He offered her his hand—it was thick, red and had a rough but creamy surface.

Stunned, Arti turned sideways and looked at him. He was made entirely of ice cream, with sunken holes for eyes and mouth. His body was made of blocks of the frozen stuff, each block a different flavour.

She suddenly couldn't help but burst into delayed laughter over the I'll-scream-Ice-cream joke.

"What? You've never seen someone made of ice cream before?"

Aarti continued laughing. "I haven't, but that's not it. I finally got the joke."

He did a sort of curtsy, using only his head.

"I'm Aarti, by the way."

"I don't have a name."

"Then I'll call you Ice Cream Boy."

He looked down at his body and then at Aarti. "That's fair."

"And lovely," Aarti smiled. "Where are you from?"

"I don't know." He looked lost. "Can I ask you something?"

"Sure." Aarti flung her extinguished cigarette butt over her shoulder.

"Can you tell me what all these colours are?" He pointed at the various chunks that made his body. "You seem to be made of shades of a single colour. I have so many."

Aarti laughed and pointed at all the chunks that made up Ice Cream Boy. "This one's obviously vanilla. This one's chocolate. I think this one's kesar, but let me check." She dipped a finger into him and he flinched. "Did that hurt?" she asked.

He shook his head. "I thought it would."

"That's mango, by the way."

"So now, we have two reds and two greens remaining."

Aarti didn't hesitate a moment before dipping her fingertips into them one after the other (since she now knew that it didn't hurt him).

"This red's watermelon, and this red is strawberry. This green is pistachio and this one's... khus?" The only time she had encountered khus before was as a green summer sharbat at her aunt's house.

"Khus, huh? So at least now I know that I must be from India."

"You don't remember where you're from?"

"All I remember is walking and snow. And then I saw this park and I just knew I was meant to be here."

Aarti had begun wondering if there was a real flesh-and-blood boy beneath the ice cream covering. But before she could ask him, he plunged his ice cream hand into the depths of his ice cream chest and pulled out a blob of vanilla and chocolate. Aarti was shocked for a moment. He stared at it and said, "So I'm made of ice cream, inside-out."

Aarti laughed. "It's actually great ice cream, better than any I've eaten before." It was even better than the ice cream she'd had with her dad once at the City Centre. The shop claimed it made the best ice cream in all of India, available in 36 flavours. "But why doesn't your ice cream feel as cold as I thought it would?" she asked.

"Did you know that ice cream sells better in the winter than in the summer?"

"I don't believe you." Aarti picked up the sheet of plastic, gave it a few shakes, and started walking back home.

"Look it up on the Internet!" he shouted behind her.

Later that night, Aarti dreamt of getting ice cream with her dad at City Centre. Ice Cream Boy stood behind the counter, passing them tiny tasting spoon after tiny tasting spoon. When they got to the fourteenth flavour, Aarti realised it was a dream. She woke up and opened the linen cupboard and took out a blanket. The noise woke her mother up. "Why are you playing drums with the cupboards in the middle of the night?"

That night was the first time since the beginning of the never-ending winter that Aarti had slept under the weight of a blanket. In the morning, when the alarm rang, she slumbered right through it.

Watching her sleep like that made her mother's eyes well up. She couldn't find it in her to wake her up. So she switched off the alarm and left for work.

PART III

Ice Cream Boy continued living in the park. Once in a while, he would venture into the nearby streets, but he always returned shortly. The kids in the neighbourhood became quite fond of him. Every morning, he stood on the footpath that ran around the periphery and stretched an arm out. The neighbourhood kids, walking down the lane on their way to school, without breaking their stride or changing direction, would bob their heads for a bite of whatever flavour of ice cream was on his tricep that day. Aarti would sit outside her house with her tea and watch this play out with a smile on her face. Then, every evening on their way back from school, the kids would discuss the ice cream dreams they had during their afternoon naps. Except for the girl with the Spider-Man school bag. In the morning, she would just walk around Ice Cream Boy, and in the evening she would trail behind the other kids and stay quiet.

One day, one of the kids began sneezing after eating the ice cream, and then returned from school with a red nose and a cold. From that day onwards, whenever Ice Cream Boy stood on the kids' route to the bus stop, the neighbourhood mothers ran behind their children to stop them from getting any ice cream. Aarti found all of this very funny and laughed even harder when her mother told her the latest on the neighbourhood grapevine: how Ice Cream Boy was spreading disease.

Aarti and her mother only spoke during dinner. Aarti's mother would give her gossip from her office or the neighbourhood. Aarti would laugh at the right points in the stories but not say a word about her own life.

•

Igloos had become all the rage at the garden parties and terrace parties of the rich and famous. Lifestyle and home improvement bloggers couldn't recommend them enough.

The identical twins on the terrace across from Aarti wanted to drink their rum in warmth and light. Their father beat them up for drawing an extension cord all the way from the fusebox on the ground floor to the terrace to fit a lamp up there, and then beat them a second time when they tried to plug a room heater into the same extension cord. So the twins were left with an oil lamp, a couple of candles for the light, and two monkey caps and two sweaters for warmth. An igloo sounded like the best option to keep both the light and the warmth trapped. That Diwali, the twins built themselves an igloo by watching how-to videos on YouTube.

Three days before the igloo was ready on the twins' terrace, Aarti bought two whole new outfits: a fresh pair of jeans, a spanking new top, and a salwar kameez. She didn't wear the salwar kameez on Diwali night like her mother asked her to. She wore her old pair of jeans with the new top though.

A few days later, when they hosted her mama for Bhai Dooj lunch, Aarti heard back from a company at which she had applied for a job. She was to start the coming Monday as a telemarketer, calling people to ask if they wanted to sell their car or buy a new secondhand vehicle.

On Monday, Vartika, the girl who sat next to her, told her—in broken fragments between dialling a number from her list, getting cussed at, and then hanging up—"You look savvy. If you play your cards right, you can get work in the banking team. But the real estate team would be totally out-of-your-league." Then she leaned towards Aarti and said, "Don't tell anybody... but they are going to give our jobs to IVR soon."

Arti wasn't sure what was happening so she asked Vartika, "Are we friends?"

Aarti felt Vartika scan her suspiciously from top to bottom. Then she threw a completely affable and welcoming smile at Aarti, and said, "Yes. We are work friends."

Aarti thanked her, made an excuse, and went to the bathroom, where she stared at herself in the mirror. Was she somebody who made friends now? She was shocked at herself, but also happy. She wanted to tell Vartika about these feelings, like friends do, but she was worried she would drive her away. So instead she kept quiet and only smiled to herself when nobody was around.

That night, Aarti did not wait for the neighbourhood to fall quiet to go for her smoke. When she got to the park, she saw that the twins had cornered Ice Cream Boy with rusted sticks of rebar in their hands. They slurred as they shouted profanities, demanding that Ice Cream Boy stop spreading disease in the neighbourhood. There were a couple of chunks of watermelon and khus on the ground, and chunks of vanilla and strawberry seekhed onto the twins' rebars. Four gaping holes in Ice Cream Boy's body stared back at Aarti. She screamed the twins' names and ran up to them in a rage. She kicked them, over and over, one after the other. Then she pulled a piece of rebar away from one of them and went to town on them with it till they scrambled back to their feet and ran away.

Ice Cream Boy picked up a large block of khus ice cream from the ground. He tried putting it back in but it refused to merge into his body. This wasn't the first time that chunks of him had been pulled out, but they had always melted back in afterwards. Together, with some effort, they managed to cram the four chunks of ice cream into their correct holes, but as soon as Ice Cream Boy took a step, they fell out again.

"Don't worry, it should grow back. At least, that's what usually happens when people eat parts of me."

Giving up, they returned to their usual bench. Aarti lit her cigarette and started to tell him everything about her meeting with Vartika. She got so lost in the excitement of having made a new friend in a brand-new place in her life that she forgot to smoke the first half of her cigarette, which became a beam of ash.

"It was like I heard a switch... No, no, I actually felt and heard a switch click inside me. Just like you do when you crack your knuckles? Except it was in my heart."

"I wouldn't know about that. I don't have knuckles. Or a heart."

"That's not the point! The point is, I became an entirely different person today." Aarti went on talking till she finished her cigarette, and then fell quiet.

After a while, she fished out a second cigarette from behind her ear. She had started smoking two every night, as her conversations with Ice Cream Boy had gotten longer. That day a hit movie was playing on cable, so the neighbourhood TV sets were blaring late; but for the first time since her father's death, Aarti felt a quiet in her head. The same head that had never stopped hearing the kerosene stove hiss, the chamcha-patila clang and the thousand whirring fans, had finally met silence.

Ice Cream Boy sat back and watched the cigarette smoke wisp into the cold air. When Aarti picked up her plastic sheet and turned to wave goodbye, she noticed that the holes in Ice Cream Boy's body had filled up with a pastel golden brown she hadn't seen before.

"What's that!"

He looked down. "Oh!"

Without checking with him first, Aarti scooped up a finger of the new ice cream and tasted it. "It's butterscotch."

"But I don't feel any different."

"Did you feel different the first time you got any of your other flavours?"

"I don't even know when I got these first seven. You know that."

"Well, I have to go brush my teeth and sleep. Tell me if you feel something in the morning."

The next morning, she made tea for her mother and herself, and sat in her usual spot outside her door. The kids were on their way to school in a straight file. Their mothers had made a barricade between their line and Ice Cream Boy. They were carrying rulers, brooms and other instruments of corporal punishment. The girl with the Spider-Man school bag, who never ate ice cream, couldn't help but take a peek at Ice Cream Boy. Ice Cream Boy smiled at her. At the sight of the butterscotch, the girl ran towards him, grabbed a fistful and ran back to the line. She had barely taken a bite when the mother closest to her delivered a rap right on her knuckles with a ruler. The ice cream fell from her hand to the ground, but the kid looked up and smiled, wearing an ice cream beard.

PART IV

The uncles and aunties of the neighbourhood Residents' Welfare Association deliberated for a while on who should get the security job of keeping the disease-causing Ice Cream Boy away from the park, and finally decided on contracting it out to the twins. The twins' parents were happy because the twins were finally making enough money to pay for their own rum and candles. The twins built themselves an igloo in the park as their guard station. They no longer drank only at night. During the day, they drank on the park bench closest to their igloo—not the one Aarti sat on at night—and watched the kids play. The uncles and aunties didn't mind their drinking; they were looking out for the kids, after all.

These measures seemed to work as intended. Ice Cream Boy only appeared at night, after the twins had passed out, when it was time for Aarti's smoke. One night, she noticed Ice Cream Boy flinching when one of the collapsed twins moved in his sleep.

Her eyes welled up on feeling Ice Cream Boy's fear. "Where do you go when I am not here?" she asked.

"Here and there."

"Why don't you try to fight back?"

He turned his two hands to point to his body. "Do you think I want parts of me strewn all around the neighbourhood?"

"Are you afraid that someday I will do that to you?"

"No. You make me feel safe."

Aarti tried to get Ice Cream Boy to go places with her, but they couldn't because he left trails of molten ice cream for everyone to clean up wherever he went. It was worse if she tried to take him to the heated indoors. Aarti and her mother had learnt that lesson when Aarti had finally found the courage to take him inside her home. Both women had spent the better part of that night wiping down every surface in the house. Ice Cream Boy had spent the night outside their gate, filled with guilt and worry. The smell of the various ice cream flavours hung around the house for weeks, and their attempts to get rid of it left the place reeking of citrus-fragrance cleaner for another month. Aarti was upset that by the time this olfactory ordeal ended, she couldn't smell her dad in the house anymore. Moreover, the cleaning required them to take down the decorations for her mother's birthday that had hung on the walls since the accident. She started sleeping in one of her dad's shirts, until finally she could only smell herself in it.

•

Vartika would repeatedly do F-L-A-M-E-S with their names, only to come to Marriage each time and tell Aarti, "See! We're soulmates. We would already be married if we weren't both straight." It made Aarti blush. That made Vartika wrap her arms around Aarti's waist, and Aarti would rest her head on Vartika's shoulder.

One day, when resting in Vartika's arms, Aarti told her, "I want you to meet Ice Cream Boy. When I spend time with both of you separately, I feel like I am two different people."

Vartika agreed to join them in the park that evening on the condition that Aarti would have a drink with her. Aarti was willing.

•

The beer bottles in Vartika's bag clinked as she hobbled out of the rickshaw in her many layers of clothing. Aarti darted home to get a couple of glasses for the beer. She wondered when Ice Cream Boy would come around.

Vartika sat on the bench hugging the bottles. The twins crawled out of their igloo with their rum. Vartika and the twins made mischievous eyes at each other. Unfortunately for them, Aarti returned to the park with the glasses just then. Aarti hurled a few choice words at the twins and they crawled back into the igloo.

"Why did you do that? They were super cute!"

"They beat up my friend."

"Why are there only two glasses? You're chickening out!"

"No, my friend doesn't drink."

"Where is he, by the way?"

"I don't know. I hope he comes by."

"Why don't you call him?"

"He doesn't have a phone."

Vartika fell silent for a moment as the gears in her mind turned. "Aarti, is your friend a poor homeless person?"

"Yes and no."

"What do you mean, yes and no? Please tell me he isn't some unbathed fakir with tatters for clothes? He'll probably be bhand on cheap weed."

"No, just wait and you'll see."

Vartika tried to drill some sense into Aarti. The crime rate had soared since the onset of the long winter. Many people had no shelter and had to find ways to survive.

They waited. The twins were playing old Rafi songs inside the igloo. When Ice Cream Boy finally arrived, Vartika could not believe that he was made entirely of ice cream.

"Can I dip my arm inside him?"

"Ask him. He's right here."

"Sure," Ice Cream Boy waved.

Vartika slipped her arm into Ice Cream Boy's stomach till it came out of the other side. She stared at him and then at Aarti and then back at him and said, "Cool!" She pulled her arm out and Aarti took her home to wash it. When they returned, Ice Cream Boy had made beer floats in the two glasses—vanilla for Aarti and butterscotch for Vartika.

Ice Cream Boy had somehow chosen butterscotch without realising that it was Vartika's favourite flavour. Vartika checked with Aarti if she told Ice Cream Boy about it and Aarti said that even she did not know.

Vartika and Ice Cream Boy got along rather well despite Aarti's suspicions. Their shenanigans included forcing Aarti to sing "Chocolate, lime juice, ice cream, toffeeyaan…" from the 90s Hindi hit *Hum Aapke Hain Koun..!* despite her protests of reluctance.

The next morning, Vartika called Aarti and told her that that night she had a dream where she was eating butterscotch ice cream with her grandparents in Shimla at a store run by Ice Cream Boy. Her grandparents had given her a lick of their brandy before taking her out to the ice cream store. Except Vartika had never been to Shimla with her grandparents. The butterscotch and brandy part was true, but it had happened when Vartika was four, in her own house, during one of the worst winters the city had seen (before the presently ongoing never-ending one.) She had been in Shimla not with her grandparents but with her parents.

Over the next few weeks, Vartika visited Ice Cream Boy with Aarti after work every day. She made sure to eat the ice cream because she wanted to have that same dream again. It made her feel protected, in a way she hadn't since she was a toddler. Meanwhile, Aarti got involved with Vartika's friend circle outside of work. She was suddenly a part of a world she wouldn't have imagined for herself in college. They went to house parties and malls. They went to the movies.

The one part which made Aarti feel like an outcast despite having been wholly accepted by the group was that all of the aforementioned hangouts involved a lot of hormonal, pheromonal young couples and their drama—triggering each other, lashing out against each other after being triggered, fighting, making up, making out and more. While Vartika always ensured she found a guy to cling to, Aarti found it increasingly awkward to be the odd-numbered wheel in an unfamiliar situation, almost always in an unfamiliar location.

Ice Cream Boy never went to any of the house parties with Aarti, but he did accompany her to one that was held on a lawn. When it started snowing and everyone went indoors, he smiled and stood outside and alone in the snow. Every now and then, Aarti checked on him through the window, and he smiled and waved. Every now and then, one of her friends came out, grabbed a few scoops of ice cream in a bowl and went back in. At one point in the night, Ice Cream Boy walked away. Aarti was deeply hurt at being abandoned like that, but she didn't say anything. On the other hand, Ice Cream Boy felt the same when Aarti left him alone outside.

The day Aarti bought a new jacket to blend in with Vartika's friends, she invited all the friends to the park for Ice Cream Boy. Not all of them showed up, but there were enough to make Ice Cream Boy feel wanted after the other night's disappointment.

For the party, one of their friends whose father owned an ice cream franchise lugged a softie machine to the park on one of his supply trucks. "Instead of just eating scoops of Ice Cream Boy, we can put the scoops in the machine and get softies." Everybody was on board, including Ice Cream Boy. When he held the extrusions produced by the softie machine, it excited him. "This is so soft and fluffy. I can't believe it's made of plain old me!"

The softies turned out to be a hit. Even the twins stepped out of the igloo and got their first taste of Ice Cream Boy in softie form. All that ice cream, along with all the vodka, whiskey and beer in the park setting, turned everyone into drunk children. Vartika wouldn't let go of the swing and made Aarti push her back and forth. Each time she fell down, she got another scoop of ice cream and ran back to the swing.

A little past midnight, many of the party started to head home. In the end, it was just Vartika, Aarti, the ice cream franchise heir, and another boy who wasn't close to anyone in the group but always stayed till the end of all their parties. The ice cream franchise heir kept trying to kiss Vartika by putting ice cream on her face and asking her if he could help clean it. The twins–guardians of the park–struggled to pull their plastic bathing tub out of the igloo. They had built the igloo around the tub and ever since then the tub had been stuck inside. They had to break a part of the igloo to pull it out, but they didn't care. All their drunkenness knew was that they wanted to have a tub full of ice cream. Except that by the time they had extricated the tub, they were exhausted, and soon passed out.

By that point in the evening, Ice Cream Boy had lost half his body mass. He was chiseled and cut in places and had holes in others. He was exhausted too, but he was having such a good time that he didn't care.

Drunk Vartika, in an attempt to dodge a softie-smearing attempt by the ice cream franchise heir, changed the topic to Ice Cream Boy. "O-M-G! He looks so odd. We have to do something. We have to give him his volume back!"

"No, it's alright," said Ice Cream Boy. "It'll all grow back in a few days. I might even get a new flavour!"

"But you look like the Pillsbury Doughboy was attacked by zombies."

Everybody laughed and Ice Cream Boy rearranged his body so that he looked more like a human and less like a half-bitten corpse. He looked at Aarti, who was passed out on her park bench with an unlit cigarette in her mouth.

"But you're so thin now," said the ice cream franchise heir. "What can we do? Can we buy milk and pour it over you?" He wanted to solve this problem fast so that he could take Drunk Vartika somewhere away from all these distractions. "Let's see if Ice Cream Boy can become Softie Boy. Right now, you're all *chunks* of ice cream. But if we use the machine then you'll become smooth and fluffy."

"No, please, don't do that. I'm not sure it will work," Ice Cream Boy protested.

Nobody cared. Ice Cream Boy screamed for help. Vartika and the franchise heir pushed him towards the softie machine. The twins woke up and joined them in helping Ice Cream Boy into the softie machine. Ice Cream Boy tried struggling, but his first attempt left his arm in the hands of one of the twins, so he stopped.

Ice Cream Boy screamed and screamed but Aarti did not wake up. Limb by limb he was lowered into the softie machine, and finally his howling head went in too. The twins placed their tub under the dispenser taps of the machine. The ice cream that came out looked very light brownish—all of Ice Cream Boy's flavours had blended into one. One of the twins tasted it.

"It doesn't taste like anything."

"It tastes like cheap mixed fruit juice with vanilla ice cream," said Vartika, spitting it out.

When all of Ice Cream Boy was in the tub, he tried to restructure himself and rise, but his new softie consistency stopped him. Each time his unformed face rose out of the lump, it collapsed back into itself. Ice

Cream Boy finally gave up on resurrection and tried just to get the holes that were his eyes and mouth working again.

Vartika went on apologising to the tub full of Ice Cream Boy and then to a sleeping Aarti. The ice cream franchise heir dragged her away from the park and into his truck. He told her they needed to get out of there as soon as possible. The twins ran back to their broken igloo. Aarti was still passed out on the bench. Worried that she might catch hypothermia, Ice Cream Boy called out to her to wake her up, but she didn't move. The energy he expended in trying to shout Aarti awake made him lose what little consistency he had mustered to keep the shape of his face. Once again, he went back to being a quiet molehill of soft serve ice cream in a tub.

Thankfully, after an hour or so, Aarti's mother woke up and called her phone. On hearing the phone ring outside in the park, she darted out to get her daughter back to warmth. She was shocked that Ice Cream Boy and Vartika had left without sending drunk Aarti home.

Aarti's mother did not say anything to her daughter the next day. She was afraid Aarti would withdraw from her even further than she already had.

Aarti, for her part, barely remembered what had happened the night before; she had blacked out.

That night, she waited for Ice Cream Boy to show up before she lit her cigarette. When he didn't show up, she started to cry. At that moment, a face formed in the tub. "Aarti?"

Aarti jumped back.

"I am sorry, it was becoming too difficult to maintain my eyes and mouth. And without my eyes I can't see."

"What happened to you?! Why are you like this in a tub?"

Ice Cream Boy told her what happened after she passed out. Aarti broke down and fell to her knees. She put her arms around the tub and wailed. As she wailed, with every passing second, the temperature started to rise. The snow in the park began to melt. So did Ice Cream Boy. His consistency became more and more liquid and it became impossible for him to retain the holes that allowed him to see and speak. It started to look like he was drowning. After she stopped, it took a few minutes for the cold to return, and an hour or so before Ice Cream Boy could gather himself enough to form a face.

PART V

Nobody touched the abandoned softie machine that stood in the middle of the park. For a few weeks, Vartika was nowhere to be found—not at work, not on the phone. Aarti couldn't reach any of their other friends, either; she didn't have their numbers. It had always been Vartika who did the planning and coordination.

Aarti asked about her at the office and was told Vartika had been AWOL. The HR department had tried to call the home number Vartika had written on her onboarding forms from when she was hired, but that number was defunct.

Aarti was in a rage over what Vartika and her friends had done to Ice Cream Boy. In her fury, she had already beaten the shit out of the twins in the middle of the park while the entire neighbourhood watched. Their mother cursed at Aarti but the twins' father clapped and asked her to beat them harder. Ice Cream Boy's face in the tub kept shouting for her to stop, but she didn't.

Aarti started to drink a quarter of rum with her two cigarettes during her night smoking sessions with Ice Cream Boy. Unlike before, when she had long conversations with him, the two stayed quiet.

Meanwhile, Ice Cream Boy had decided he would have to separate his flavours before trying to rebuild his anthropomorphic body. Every night, he worked at splitting them and keeping them apart. Aarti would watch as blobs of different flavours formed along the circumference of the tub. For the first few days, the flavours blended right back in.

By the time Ice Cream Boy could keep them all separated, Aarti's daily intake of rum had increased to half a bottle and the two nightly cigarettes had become five. Ice Cream Boy's softie consistency started to return to its older, chunkier form. He found it easier to assemble a head using the different flavours, and stick up out of the tub to talk.

Aarti kept checking social media, but there had been no activity on any of Vartika's accounts. She tried to remember where Vartika's friends worked, but she mostly remembered wrong—except for two people. She went to the first person's office. That friend told her that nobody had seen or heard from Vartika since the night at the park. Next she went to the ice cream franchise heir's shop and got his number. The ice cream franchise heir told Aarti that he didn't think Vartika wanted to be friends with her anymore.

"That's how she is," he said. "She uses you and then she dumps you."

"Nonsense."

"I haven't heard from her either and I treated her like a queen. You have any idea how much I've spent on her?"

"It's not just us; nobody has heard from her! Aren't you worried that something has happened to her?"

"Forget about Vartika. Make new friends and stop calling me!" He hung up, and when Aarti tried calling him again, he didn't pick up.

Then, one night, when Aarti got to the park with her rum and cigarettes, she saw Vartika sitting on the bench, leaning forward and talking to Ice Cream Boy. Aarti ran to the bench and pushed Vartika to the ground. "Don't fucking touch him!"

Ice Cream Boy screamed, "Stop it, Aarti!"

"She turned you into this! Her and her friends!" yelled Aarti. She stared down at Vartika, whose face looked swollen and red with remorse.

"Look at me, Aarti, look at me!" Ice Cream Boy called out.

When Aarti turned, she saw a miniature version of Ice Cream Boy, in his original multi-flavour avatar, standing ankle-deep in the tub full of ice cream. She was stumped. Ice Cream Boy smiled.

"Vartika came up with this idea. Instead of trying to rise up and become all of myself again, I could be a smaller version of myself."

"And then he can continue to absorb more of himself through his legs and keep growing a little bit at a time," Vartika added.

"That's how plants and animals grow, she said!"

Aarti broke into tears. Her brain stopped processing anything that the two of them said. Instead, it kept repeating: *Cytoplasm, nucleoplasm, mitochondrion, Golgi apparatus, ribosomes, lysosomes, peroxisome, vacuole...*

Vartika got back up, dusted the snow off her pants and elbows, and held Aarti in her arms like she always used to. Aarti dropped her head to her shoulder just like before. Vartika's mouth formed a small smile when she felt Aarti's warm tears fall onto her collarbone. Her arms shook as Aarti lay in them, sobbing. A lump started to form inside Vartika's throat, and after a moment, she broke down too. "I'm sorry, I'm sorry..." She went on apologising. Ice Cream Boy melted back into the tub to give them some space. (Not that he couldn't hear them.)

"Why did you do it?"

"I'm sorry... I'm really, really sorry..."

The crying stopped. Their faces were red, eyes swollen, and teardrops stung their unchapped lips.

"Where were you all these days?"

Vartika burst into another heart-wrenching cry. Aarti wrapped herself completely around Vartika, pushing one hand into her hair and the other pushing Vartika's face onto her shoulder. The way their bodies shifted against each other made it the first time that Aarti was comforting Vartika, rather than the other way around.

"I ran, you know. As soon as the truck door opened, I ran and I ran and I didn't stop. I promise, I didn't." Vartika continued sobbing.

The two sat down. Aarti lit two cigarettes, the same way Vartika used to do for her. Vartika told her about the night she and the ice cream franchise heir had abandoned Ice Cream Boy and Aarti in the park. At some point on their drunken truck drive away, she felt his gaze–and the way he gripped her wrist–change from those of a charismatic rebel to those of a malignant tyrant.

"I froze when it happened. Then when I was running, I threw my SIM. I thought he would track me. Here, save my new number." She called Aarti's phone from hers. Vartika and Aarti did not open the bottles of rum they had each brought to the park. They finished one full pack of cigarettes between them by the time it was morning. Vartika tried offering Ice Cream Boy a drag for which she got a reprimanding look from Aarti.

"You don't know this but I don't breathe," said Ice Cream Boy. "The eye holes do their function and I can see. The mouth hole is for talking. But there are no nostrils on my face."

"How do you smell?"

"Just like how I listen. Through the outer layer of my ice cream flesh."

The next week, Vartika got a job at one of the "stone ice cream" places that seemed to be a blooming trend. The gratuitous violence of making ice cream by beating it to shit on a stone slab with blades appealed to Vartika deeply. Every night after work, she hung out with Aarti and Ice Cream Boy at the park and sometimes crashed at Aarti's.

One day, Vartika brought a container of cookies and cream to the park. She said to Aarti and Ice Cream Boy, "What if we tried thickening him by adding ice cream? I beat it together myself." Aarti was worried, but Ice Cream Boy was open to trying anything that could help him grow back to his original size. So the girls scooped every last bit of the cookies and cream from the container into Ice Cream Boy's tub. Ice Cream Boy sank back into the tub, mixed himself together, and rose back into his usual shape. The cookies and cream had found its place as a giant chunk in his form. Except, just as the three of them began cheering, the block of cookies and cream dropped out of him and fell onto the ground. Vartika started crying immediately. Ice Cream Boy and Aarti had to spend the rest of the evening explaining to her that this didn't mean that Ice Cream Boy was rejecting her or that they would stop loving her.

PART VI

Aarti's father's 12th death anniversary had just passed. Ice Cream Boy had managed to grow back to his full size and finally stepped out of the tub. Chunks of a new flavour had appeared on his body—gulkand. It was the third texture among the nine flavours. The mango and watermelon had the texture of a natural sorbet; the other ice creams were creamy. Gulkand was creamy too, but with soft bumps of candied, shredded rose petals.

The first thing that Ice Cream Boy did with his newfound mobility was to go from house to house announcing, "I am fine now! I am free now!" He let the kids in each house get a scoop or two to celebrate.

The twins had fixed the abandoned softie machine and used it to set up an ice cream stall of their own in the park. Ice Cream Boy contributed the "seed fund" for the twins' ice cream machine by allowing them to scoop parts of him to make softies. The neighbourhood encouraged the business run by their local drunks, and the adults would show up in the afternoons and after dinner to grab a cup or a cone. The kids, though, still preferred to get their ice cream straight from the source, rather than the machine-softened version.

The uncles and aunties would have ice cream dreams like the others, but their morning anxieties ensured that most of them did not remember the dreams. The few of them who did remember told the others, who refused to believe that Ice Cream Boy had anything to do with it.

Soon the twins were able to run the business without contributions from Ice Cream Boy. But customers started to complain in person and on social media that the ice cream did not taste the same. They had stopped having dreams that healed their inner child. The twins' online ratings dropped from a 4.8 to a 3.9. So they soon went back to adding a couple of scoops of Ice Cream Boy to the ingredients before loading them into the machine. The complaints stopped, and their ratings climbed back to 4.6.

•

At work, Vartika gave her number to cute customers with their orders, and some of them called her. She spent a lot of time talking to them at night but blocked their numbers any time any of them tried to take the relationship beyond phone sex.

Aarti joined the group of friends that Vartika made through her new job. When Aarti first met Vartika's work-bestie's brother Brijesh, a puddle formed under her armpits. As she sniffed the puddle under her arm, she was intoxicated by the sweetest vanilla scent she had ever smelled. It reminded her of the first night she'd met Ice Cream Boy, when even before she'd laid eyes on him, she could smell vanilla everywhere.

She met Brijesh often in a group, but they never exchanged a word. Aarti, who had never been much of a talker in group settings, found herself becoming even quieter. Instead of following the conversation going on in the group, she spent most of her silence high on the smell of vanilla that Brijesh infused in her senses.

In the week before Holi, Brijesh sent Aarti his first text to her individual number (rather than addressing everyone in the group chat). Aarti, excited, told Vartika. Vartika waved it off. "He texts everyone." But soon Aarti and Brijesh started to meet every single day after work—and only some of those times were with the group. She would still not say a word to him when they were with the others, though she'd let him sit or stand next to her with the sides of their bodies touching. However, every night, Aarti would quickly finish her nightly smoke with Vartika and Ice Cream Boy and then run home to talk to Brijesh till one of them fell asleep. The casual conversations and light flirting paved its way to the edges of phone sex, where words were lost. A tense silence where both of them made light, suggestive noises but neither wanted to start saying the sexy parts. During these moments, Aarti found her senses utterly overwhelmed by the essence of vanilla. Her lungs filled up with the scent, the taste and texture flooding her mouth, the cold touch of vanilla ice cream all over her body. She even saw swirls of creamy white when she closed her eyes.

Soon enough, she made sure she spoke to Brijesh every morning on his commute to work, again on his commute from the office to meet her, and once more when he was on his way home.

In the fervour of anticipation of these calls, she had stopped noticing anything happening with Vartika and Ice Cream Boy. One day, Vartika asked Ice Cream Boy if she could take a few bricks of ice cream from him. Bigshots from her store's corporate office were going to be making their rounds and she wanted to leave them blown away– "Which, let's be honest," she said, "is not going to be possible with the quality of ice cream we have." Ice Cream Boy obliged. The flavour chunks that made up his body were constantly moving in a slow convection; the vanilla Vartika wanted was currently spread over his shoulder and neck. Vartika took out the chunk and placed it in a container branded with her company's logo. After she was done, Ice Cream Boy looked like a huge vampire had taken a bite out of him.

The day after Vartika took the ice cream, Brijesh told Aarti that their "relationship had matured". To celebrate that, he bought her cheap but colourful earrings. This was Aarti's first romantic gift. Her senses filled up all over again with the same intoxicating high-grade vanilla that she smelled when Brijesh and her had phone sex. She couldn't contain herself. She had an intense physical reaction that made her grab Brijesh and kiss him. Tears drenched the first kiss of her life. The inside of Brijesh's mouth unsurprisingly tasted of vanilla. The longer she kissed him, the taste grew more and more intense until it got as bitter as concentrated essence. When she pulled away, Brijesh smiled and asked her, "How was it for you?" She blushed, relished the lingering bitterness on the inside of her mouth, and proceeded to try on the gift earrings. They took a selfie together and she posted it on her stories. Vartika replied to the story: "I can see you drooling from the corner of your mouth! You kissed Brijesh!"

The next morning, Aarti was woken up by Vartika incessantly calling her phone. "Go outside!"

"What happened?"

"Just go outside."

"Okay, okay, give me a minute. I'll call you back."

Aarti's mother saw her awake. "Have you seen the news?"

World over, the snow and ice had developed patches of different colours. The colours moved in slow convection, just as they did on Ice Cream Boy. The news reported that the coloured ice was flavoured. Aarti ran out to see. She found Ice Cream Boy standing against a backdrop that looked exactly like him.

•

After the colours refused to return to the pristine white of the snow, the UN embraced the phenomenon as a sign from nature to remember the colours of summer. On April Fool's Day, they announced May 2nd to be World Summer Remembrance Day. After a couple of weeks of international confusion as to whether this was an April Fools prank or not, all the nations accepted World Summer Remembrance Day as an international holiday.

Brijesh called Aarti to tell her that he was going away for a few days. His work friends were going to take advantage of the extra holiday and make a trip to the closest hill station. Aarti said she was okay with it, as long as he would talk to her on the phone throughout the journey, and again on his way back.

Brijesh protested. "Now that our relationship is mature, now that I got you a gift and you kissed me, we don't need to talk all the time. We should be allowed to take breaks."

Aarti lashed out at him: "Our kisses only taste bitter to me."

This conversation escalated into their first fight, which went on for a few days across private texts, calls, passive aggressive group texts and in-person meetings. On the night before Brijesh's outing, when Aarti wouldn't cave, Brijesh called her a psycho, hung up and switched off his phone. Aarti's heart was pounding. She tried calling him again and again, only to keep hearing the electronic lady telling her that the phone was switched off. She felt something rise from the pit of her stomach till she was puking, her mouth flooded with the vanilla bitterness.

The next day it snowed heavily. It became one of the few heavy snow days when people were out on the streets, because they couldn't get enough of the free street ice cream. When Aarti tried the street ice cream, all she could taste was the bitterness in her mouth. She thought that perhaps a scoop of Ice Cream Boy might cleanse her palate, but even that failed. She accused Ice Cream Boy of adulterating himself with the twins' ice cream products.

Brijesh did not call or message Aarti even once. Aarti's eyes started to burn when it was time for her to clock out of work. She heard the voice of her teenage self, repeating: *Cytoplasm, nucleoplasm, mitochondrion, Golgi apparatus, ribosomes, lysosomes, peroxisome, vacuole…* To shut the voice down, she decided to stay at work late and call some more numbers from her list. It took people by surprise to receive marketing calls so late in the evening, and so Aarti was able to make two sales—a two-wheeler loan and a vacation loan.

When her mother called her to ask if she should wait for her to eat dinner, Brijesh still hadn't called. The voice of teenage Aarti kept getting louder and louder in her head. She tried calling Brijesh but he didn't pick up. After she got screamed at four times for interrupting people's dinner to sell them loans, she logged out of her machine. She banged her headset down so hard that it snapped. She fished out her bottle of rum from her bag, looked around to check if anyone was watching her, and then gulped down half of the quarter. Soon drunk, Aarti typed six different messages to Brijesh ranging from abject grovels to murderous threats, but deleted them all before sending. She glued the broken headset back together. Her eyes welled up with tears, but she didn't let a single drop roll down her red cheeks. Her entire being was quaking with rage. She walked back home in the snow with the edges of her jacket sleeves balled into her fists.

By the time a snow-covered, quarter-bottle-down Aarti reached her neighbourhood, it had stopped snowing. She reached the park to find Ice Cream Boy and Vartika sitting face to face on the same bench where Aarti and Ice Cream Boy had first met. Vartika and Ice Cream Boy were excited because a new pastel purple-coloured flavour had grown in the space left behind by the ice cream that Vartika had taken. Vartika pushed a finger into his shoulder and scooped some out to taste it. "It's black currant!"

The snow on Aarti's hair and shoulders started to melt. Vapours emanated from her with a hiss and a sizzle. Vartika stopped scooping fingerfuls and sunk her jaws into Ice Cream Boy's shoulder. Aarti's eyes widened and she let out a scream.

The weather had flipped like a switch. It turned hot and dry, like a summer night. The snow around them started to melt and so did Ice Cream Boy. In her screaming rage, Aarti ran to the two of them, wrapped her arms around Vartika and pulled her away. She kicked Ice Cream Boy, lodging her foot right into his stomach. When she pulled her foot out, she fell backwards onto Vartika. A chunk of ice cream came out with her foot.

The sudden spike in heat had woken up the entire neighbourhood. People opened their windows and looked out. One of the twins was half-way out the broken archway of their melting igloo. But just as Aarti stopped screaming, the temperature dropped right back to freezing, and it started to snow again. Everything that had been melting froze again in that very fraction of a second. The twin had his ass caught under the collapsing but frozen igloo entrance.

Aarti curled up in a fetal position on the ground where she was and closed her eyes. Ice Cream Boy and Vartika scrambled over to her. Vartika tried to help Aarti up but she wouldn't budge. So she sat down next to her and placed Aarti's head in her lap. Ice Cream Boy sat on the other side.

"I think Brijesh is dead." Aarti's body was rigid, her fists clenched.

"What?!"

"I told him to call me and he called me a psycho. Now he isn't answering his phone or looking at his texts."

"Boys are dicks. Don't worry, let's get some ice cream. We have black currant now!"

"Brijesh is dead, I'm telling you! He died in an accident when he went out with his friends. I knew he was going to die if he didn't talk to me."

"Let me call him," said Vartika.

Understanding that Aarti was actually fine, just heartbroken, Ice Cream Boy looked down to examine the hole in his torso that Aarti's foot had left. Something felt different this time.

A drunk and slurring Brijesh picked up Vartika's call. "Your friend is a psycho!"

Aarti broke into tears on hearing his voice on speakerphone. She grabbed Vartika's phone. "I love you, I love you so much. Please don't die."

"Fuck off, psycho." He hung up.

Aarti couldn't stop crying. Vartika signalled Ice Cream Boy to help Aarti up. Ice Cream Boy wasn't paying attention. He was trying to will the hole to fill itself up, as had happened most times before. But this time, it wasn't working. Vartika snapped at him and his mind returned to the situation at hand. He helped Vartika prop Aarti up and they got back to their bench.

After the girls left, Ice Cream Boy kept staring at the parts they had eaten off of him. Only after he saw the bumps carved out by their spoons fill themselves up did he relax and let his shoulders drop. He hoped the chunk Aarti had kicked out would grow back too.

The next morning, Aarti woke up to a message from Brijesh that said, "Break up. Stop calling me."

Aarti felt the bitterness pool in her mouth. Her lungs choked as the sweet scent became so intense it turned pungent. The cold texture of ice cream that had soothed her body on the day they kissed started to feel like frostbite. Aarti puked again and dropped next to her bed in a fetal position.

The next morning, the news reported that the colours and flavours in the snowscape had disappeared. The people mourned their loss.

•

Vartika's intervention did not help Brijesh change his mind. His friends had told him that a girl who couldn't stop calling him would only cause problems later. All of the others had had girlfriends who had threatened to commit suicide before—or worse, attacked them with knives or scissors or even chair parts for "small things" like WhatsApping with another girl or posting fire emojis on a girl's thirst trap pictures.

Vartika fought hard for Aarti, telling Brijesh that Aarti was not one of those girls. But even the other girls in their group were on Brijesh's side. The leader of the girls' group told Vartika, "Aarti and Brijesh just have to be friends. Or she should leave the group. We can't have this drama."

A month or so into the return of the flavourless snowscape, governments across the world announced a ten-million-dollar prize for anyone who could bring the colours and flavours back. Every leader, godman, and tech billionaire announced a soon-to-come solution.

Meanwhile, Aarti found that her senses were not being assaulted by vanilla quite so often or so strongly. However, the bitterness kept pooling in her mouth till she had to puke. She tried her best to keep washing her mouth, but at least twice a day she would forget, and then she would throw up.

She went to work for a couple of days, but since she couldn't stop puking and crying, she decided to call in sick. She missed work all through HR's fitness week initiative at the office, staying in her room all day and only stepping out to meet Ice Cream Boy and Vartika at night. All this while, she did not notice that the hole she had kicked out of Ice Cream Boy hadn't filled itself up again.

•

The day the twins decided to create their own savory ice cream flavours, Vartika and Aarti were smoking on the bench. Ice Cream Boy was helping the twins set up tasting trays for their new menu. Their first batch was called "masala box" and included chaat masala, chilli, dhaniya-jeera and oregano (because they loved pizza).

When Ice Cream Boy passed the tasters to Aarti, she suddenly noticed the hole.

"Is this from that night?" she asked.

Ice Cream Boy nodded and offered the tray of tasters to Vartika.

"I'm sorry," she said.

"It's okay." He turned to walk back to the twins. Aarti grabbed his wrist to stop him. He stopped and said, "It's okay, Aarti. Shit happens. Please let go of my hand."

"No. Sit with me. It has been ages since we've spoken." She held his wrist tighter.

As Ice Cream Boy pulled away, his arm came detached. His hand fell to the floor, leaving his ice cream wrist in her hand. Ice Cream Boy panicked. He dropped to the floor, picked up his hand and frantically tried to reconnect it with his forearm.

"What's wrong? It'll grow back, na?"

"Hold that wrist piece between them, please." Ice Cream Boy was barely able to speak, his voice choking.

Aarti followed his instruction. The arm, the wrist piece and the palm were held together. Ice Cream Boy stared at the edges of the pieces, trying to will them to reconnect. Vartika and the twins joined them.

The warmth of their bodies allowed for some of the ice cream to melt and the pieces looked like they were starting to come back together. Ice Cream Boy heaved a sigh of relief. The others took their cues from him and sighed too. "I think we're fine now."

But the moment everyone let go, the two parts fell right to the ground. Before anyone could react, one of the twins asked Ice Cream Boy, "Can we take these two chunks for the softie machine?"

Ice Cream Boy shrugged.

"What is happening?!" Aarti shouted at Ice Cream Boy. The realisation that she had been so self-absorbed in her heartbreak that she hadn't noticed the persistent gaping hole in Ice Cream Boy's body caused her pain she wasn't ready for. So she lashed out at everyone for not telling her, and stormed off to the first wine shop she could find. A couple of shots down, at the standing table in the garage full of strangers behind the wine shop, her heart sank as she realised that she'd been involved in both the accidents—the hole in the stomach and the loss of the arm.

PART VII

Aarti often woke up crying from heartbreak, and on those days she missed work. She had developed a tolerance for the bitterness in her mouth and had stopped puking. The added guilt and shame of hurting Ice Cream Boy, her first real friend, broke her in ways she was not familiar with. Whenever she missed puking, she would drink till it all came right back up, and then pass out from exhaustion and borderline alcohol poisoning. She could barely get herself to do any work, either. On the days she managed to drag herself to the office, she would barely manage one or two calls before she began to drink, and then she would start slurring her words. Soon, she was fired.

But every time she cried, the global temperatures rose by a tiny fraction of a degree. Scientists the world over tried in vain to understand what was causing these small rises. By the time Aarti was done grieving the breakup and did not need to puke again, the world was 0.57 degrees warmer than it had been before.

The governments, tech billionaires, and religious leaders claimed responsibility for the rising temperatures. Everyone was saving the world, and every saviour had die-hard followers who sometimes broke into fights over the claims made by their leaders. Some fought in the comments sections and threads of social media posts and others fought in the streets. Some conflicts were only verbal; others got violent. On the day one of the many groups of supremacists bombed a mall to stake their claim of their leader being responsible for the rise in temperature, Aarti started looking for another job.

At the park, the twins had put up a life-size cutout of their family's favourite godman, posing as the saviour of the world. At first they didn't want to, but their mother had beaten them till they did want to. Their ice cream shop, previously known simply as "the ice cream shop in the park", was now named after the godman.

Aarti, Vartika, and Ice Cream Boy continued to hang out at the park. Ice Cream Boy walked away from any conversation about the parts of him that wouldn't grow back. He had stopped contributing ice cream to the twins' shop or letting anyone feed off of him, out of fear of losing more body mass. Once in a while, the neighbourhood kids would surround him and drown him with their chorus of "please, please, please!" and he would relent and let them take a few bites. Then he would spend the next few hours alone, staring anxiously at the dents in his body. Once they had filled back up, he would relax and sit back, basking for a while in relief that he wasn't losing himself, and then return to the others. Still, his old jovial mood was now rarely seen. Aarti, Vartika, and even the twins felt a void of psychic energy when they were around him. They were used to Ice Cream Boy actively listening, and-then?-ing, yes-and?-ing their stories and antics. Now, all Ice Cream Boy did was make a solemn face and nod.

One evening, Vartika did not make it to the park due to a family gathering. The twins were asleep in their igloo after a particularly exhausting day selling ice cream. Aarti walked to the park for a smoke and saw Ice Cream Boy sitting alone on their bench. He looked exhausted. The elbow of one hand and the stump of the other rested on his thighs, holding up his hunched-over upper body. He did not notice Aarti walk towards the bench. The moment he felt her sit down, he jumped right up and asked her, "Would you like some ice cream?"

There was a pause. Aarti looked at him, not knowing what to say. Ice Cream Boy fumbled, "I mean… From the machine. Not from me."

"No, it's alright. I'm just here for a smoke." She lit her cigarette.

"Okay," said Ice Cream Boy. He started walking to the machine.

"Where are you going? Come, sit with me."

"Not today. I need to clean the machine." Both of them knew this was a ridiculous excuse; any attempt by Ice Cream Boy to clean anything could only end up with the thing getting covered in melted ice cream.

"I can give you company while you clean."

"No, I'll manage." He continued walking away from her.

"But I want to." Aarti got up and walked towards him.

"It's late." Ice Cream Boy unplugged the ice cream machine. "And I am tired."

"So you don't have to talk. Just listen." Aarti picked up a rag and started to wipe the machine. She was scrubbing with the same hand that held her cigarette, and the rag kept bumping the glowing tip. Embers from the cigarette fell and sizzled against the snow. She switched hands.

"I really don't want to." Ice Cream Boy placed himself between the machine and her rag. "Can you just go home? Please."

"So you also think I'm a psycho now?"

Ice Cream Boy gave up arguing with Aarti. He turned around and started walking towards the park gate. Aarti ran ahead and stood in his path. The closer he got to her, the more she walked backwards.

"Why didn't you tell me that you weren't growing those parts back?" She stopped in her steps.

Ice Cream Boy didn't say a word. He walked around her and she followed him.

"We used to tell each other everything."

"No. You told *me* everything. I didn't have anything to say to you."

"Why didn't you?"

"I don't know anything to say to you." He turned around, spread his one-and-a-half arms wide. "This—this park—is all that I know. These people are all that I know. You are all that I know. And you know it all."

"You could have still told me."

Ice Cream Boy turned around once again and started walking to the gate. In a rage, Aarti jumped forward and stubbed her cigarette out on his back. She felt the cigarette being sucked out from between her fingers; the ice cream swallowed the cigarette whole. Ice Cream Boy let out a small scream, then a choking sound. He gacked and spat out the cigarette from his mouth hole. Then, without saying a word, he continued walking to the exit.

She followed him out in silence, seething. She stopped at the footpath and kept repeating, "Talk to me. Talk to me! Come back. Talk to me!" in a louder and louder voice. Her tone slowly shifted from dry rage to damp grief. Her voice carried through the silence of the night, sending shivers down the bodies of everyone who was tucked in their beds. Many kids and even some adults found themselves starting to weep and sob as her voice rang in their ears.

The temperature started to rise again. A slow trickle of water could be heard as fresh snowmelt dripped into the sewers.

Right about when Ice Cream Boy reached the part of the lane where Aarti's father had been run over by the truck, she screamed and charged towards him with her hands outstretched in front of her. When she collided with him, her palms went right through his chest, dislodging his head and shoulders from his body. They fell to the ground, half his head splayed open at the edge of the footpath.

Aarti froze for a second. She lost her voice. All that stood before her was a torso and legs.

"Go away!" his muffled voice screamed from the ground.

She dropped to her knees and grabbed his shoulders to lift him up, but his flattened head fell from the neck, and was further deformed as it hit the ground again. His mouth tried to make words but all that came out was a low-pitched garble.

When her shock wore off, she screamed. The twins woke up. Her mother came running out their door to the street. Aarti's fists had sunk into Ice Cream Boy's shoulders as they had started to melt in her hands. It was getting hotter and hotter. The entire neighbourhood was awake, throwing off thick blankets and taking off their sweaters, opening their windows so they wouldn't suffocate in their heated rooms.

The tears rolling down Aarti's cheeks evaporated before they reached her jawline. The snow and ice that did not have time to become water just sublimated. Aarti's mother's shawl and the twins' monkey caps caught fire. For the first time in over a decade, one could see the black tar of the roads. Aarti would not stop crying.

Ice Cream Boy started flowing away with the water. Aarti chased the rivulets of cream that ran around her. Her mother stopped her before she followed a thick stream of cream into the sewer. She pulled Aarti away and held her. Aarti collapsed to the ground. Her mother dropped to her knees to keep holding onto her. Aarti stopped screaming, but continued to sob, curling up in her mother's arms.

The fires started to die down and the heat started to dissipate, but Aarti's sobs kept the weather simmering. The only sounds to be heard in the neighbourhood were of people heaving and crying, their hajaar fans starting to spin again, and a faint hiss of water evaporating from every surface that had once been covered in snow.

Aarti's mother and the twins helped her get back home, where she crashed on her bed. Her mother sat next to her, stroking her hair, as Aarti fell deeper and deeper into sleep. Outside, gentle rain cooled off a world that had become as hot as a furnace.

Aarti dreamed of getting ice cream with her dad at City Centre. There, in the dream, is where she saw Ice Cream Boy for the last time. He stood behind the counter passing them tiny tasting spoon after tiny tasting spoon.

EPILOGUE

Vartika parked herself on the store counter and drank melted ice cream from a cup. Aarti, dressed in the same server's uniform as Vartika, worked a mop on the floor. There had been a huge ice cream spill. An earthquake in the city had knocked out an entire power grid, and their ice cream shop had lost power at night. All of the ice cream was either warm milk in tubs or in a giant puddle across the floor.

"Are you going to join me?"

"I wanna have one more of these ice cream milks."

"You know they'll be spoiled by now, right?"

"That only happens if you use natural ingredients." Vartika tapped an empty cup. "This stuff here is made of pure synthetic ingredients. Drowning in preservatives. So I'm good." She tilted her head back and did a shot of yet another ice cream cup.

Aarti shook her head and continued working the mop.

"You know the last time we had a spill like this was the night the neverending winter ended? I spent three days cleaning the place up. Because it wasn't just ice cream flooding the floor. There was a dead rat floating in it. Right about here."

Aarti shook her head once again. The voice in her head recited the parts of the cell on repeat: *Cytoplasm, nucleoplasm, mitochondrion, Golgi apparatus, ribosome, lysosome, peroxisome, vacuole...*

The Legend of Rani Grace

Rashmi Ruth Devadasan

Most small towns have one unique thing they can take pride in. One specialty that belongs to that place alone, that can't be found anywhere else in the world. A unique type of halwa, the softest lungis, or a specific kind of rose milk with a GI tag.

But Puthuyirpet had nothing like that to boast about.

It was a town with a power plant and a population of people that hardly ever left. Most of the inhabitants worked at the power plant. On their days off, the townsfolk would picnic with their families at the base of the gentle Khatarnaak Falls, which fell into the graceful Nagin River—so named for the way it sinuously carved its way around the border of town.

Rani Grace was the town's gravedigger. It was a job she inherited from her mother. How did that come to pass in an otherwise quiet, mostly traditional place like Puthuyirpet? Well, someone had to bury the dead, and when Rani Grace's grandfather died it fell on her young mother to do what had to be done. At first the people in the town were shocked at having a woman gravedigger. There was lots of loose talk and a council meeting was held. But since no one else came forward to take on the task…

The Grace family home was a modest two-bedroom house built with laterite bricks. It stood at the top of a hill whose gentle slopes were dotted with the graves of people who had died as long as 250 years ago.

Rani Grace was quite comfortable with death. After all, she had been around it since she was six months old. Her mother had strapped baby Rani Grace to her back in a hardy cotton dupatta and hummed *"Laila oh Laila"* as she dug into the earth to make a rectangular hole that would receive, the next day, a person who was no more. Baby Rani Grace liked the movements of her mother's strong body as she worked—scooping up load after load of loose, damp, fragrant soil and making a large neat mound of it to the side.

Once, at age two, Rani Grace had fallen with a gentle *dhap!* four feet down onto the lid of a coffin that had been placed there just an hour and a half before. Her mother, who had been about to start covering it with earth, had just turned around for a moment to make sure she had brought the right shovel when Rani Grace had furiously waddled to the edge and tipped over. She didn't cry; instead she righted herself into a sitting position, and began giggling and playing with the damp soil that had been thrown in as a last farewell by the friends and relatives of the deceased.

As a girl, she always wore the same outfit: single-color knee-length kurtas with long sleeves folded up to the elbow, and khaki trousers—the former from Khadi Bhavan, the latter from the military surplus store in the next big town. Her hair was thick and short.

By far her most favourite thing to do was to practice digging graves by night while listening to '70s Ilaiyaraaja hits on her Walkman.

On full moon nights when she had finished her daily digging riyaz, she would lie down on the damp earth at the bottom of the hole she'd just dug and stare up at the complete moon in its perfectly rectangular frame. Nothing could top this simple pleasure.

At school she was quiet and solitary—not because she was shunned or anything filmy like that. After all, everyone in the town knew what an important, indispensable component of Puthuyirpet Rani Grace and her mother were.

It was just that Rani Grace was not a "people person".

For her sixteenth birthday—when most of her peers either got a bicycle, or if they were more well-off, a scooter—Rani Grace was presented with her first spade. She got up at 5:30 a.m. and went out to do her brisk walking *chakkar* up and down the slope of the hill, zigging and zagging between the few hundred headstones. When she came back home for breakfast, there it was on the table, wrapped in old National Geographic covers that her mother had meticulously stitched together to make a very large piece of wrapping paper, the size of a single bedsheet. Rani Grace's mother was not just a master gravedigger; she was also a consummate craftsperson.

Rani Grace's mother stood by the kitchen door watching her daughter with a serene smile. She had been feeling unusually tired this past week. *Age catching up, that's all,* she thought. She was proud of her child, who at sixteen could dig a grave just as well as she could.

Rani Grace of course knew at sight what was in the package, but that did not make her excitement sluggish. She sat down at the table and pulled it towards her. She liked how the handle felt through the wrapping.

She carefully unwrapped it and gave a barely audible gasp. It was a fine, full-sized spade. The neck was made from solid, well-aged teak wood. The handle was carved from the femur of a water buffalo, with Rani Grace's name inlaid in the bone in pure silver. The metal blade itself was molded and shaped from top quality steel made by Shazia Bi, her mother's friend, who ran a foundry on the outskirts of Puthuyirpet. The relationship between metalworker and gravedigger was forged on trust and mutual respect of each other's uncompromising dedication to their individual professions, and on the unspoken solidarity of women in vocations usually reserved for men.

Rani Grace wrapped her hands around the wooden handle. This was *her* spade, made for *her*; she could feel it in her soul. She carefully raised it above her head. She could feel its energy surge through her. Outside, thunder sounded and lightning flashed across the sky. It was mid-April, a month known for its out-of-the-blue summer storms.

Rani Grace rushed out of the house whooping, and why not? She was sixteen, she had just gotten the best gift ever, and it was raining after a whole month of heat and humidity. She ran down the hill towards the old jamun tree at the center of the hill of graves.

When she was a meter away from it, the ground gave way beneath her feet, and she fell.

At first she dropped so fast she almost stopped breathing. She was in such shock that she couldn't even scream or cry out.

As she kept falling, she felt the pace of her descent shift into a steady downward cruising speed. She found that she could change her position in mid-air, so she righted herself. She brought her legs together and held the spade with both hands in front of her body, like a knight holding a sword.

She began to think a fast-moving, psychedelic kaleidoscope of thoughts. It started with *maybe this is how I die*. Then she wished she could have given her mother one last hug before she had left the house. A smile broke across her face at the irony of her birthday also becoming her death day, and she wondered for how many people that happened.

Then, without any advance notice, she gently hit the ground. She fell to a crouch and stood up.

She was standing in a large underground cavern. Its floor was strewn with bones. Strange-looking plants grew from the cracks between them, shrubs and bushes that glowed eerily. They had succulent leaves that gave off a shimmer, like live coals. The flowers had petals with serrated edges that whipped out like sinuous blades. The thick stems were covered with eight-inch menacing-looking needles that were slowly moving, pushing out and retracting.

The walls of this subterranean chamber were covered in what looked like a spongy coat of moss—but instead of green, it was the color of clotted blood. There were also vines growing across the floor. These were a baingan-purple color, as thick as commercial shipping ropes. As they rustled and twisted, Rani Grace saw that the vines sported razor sharp black thorns, which resembled the dorsal fins of sharks sticking out of the water.

At the center of it all stood a rooster the size of an autorickshaw. It had kohl-black feathers that shone like satin. The intense black plumage of its tail would have made a peacock's multi-colored feathers look plain in comparison. The rooster stood still, its eyes like black glass beads so dark that even the flare from an acetylene torch wouldn't have brought a flicker of light into them.

The only glimmer that broke through the bird's blackness was a red glow that came on and off from deep inside its chest, like the moving beacon of a lighthouse. Rani Grace realised that this light was the glow of the creature's large pulsating heart.

On top of the fowl, sitting sideways, was a man who looked, at first glance, like somebody's Uncle. He was middle-aged and not very tall. His shape was well-rounded, like a prize Imam Pasand mango, and he was dressed in the sort of cement-grey safari suit that had been considered high fashion in the 1970s. He had a head of tightly spiralling black curls, parted on the left: thick locks that coiled and twisted like moving tentacles.

His face was like a hologram. If you tilted your head slightly one way, he looked like a jolly, clean shaven desi Santa Claus; but if you changed the angle of your gaze ever so slightly, it made his face look demonic and villainous.

He had eight hands in total, four on each side. Each wrist was adorned with a two-inch-wide gold watch.

He wore black Bata sandals. His feet seemed to have too many toes.

"Hello! Hello, ma!" he said in a voice both sweet and dangerous, like someone offering you a spoon of fresh kesari that you know for certain is poisoned. "All okay? You didn't hurt yourself, no, when you fell?"

Rani Grace didn't know whether to laugh or scream. She heard herself say "I'm fine."

"*Appada!* Excellent! Now, dear please sit. *Utkaranga!* Please sit."

From beneath her, just behind her bum, an inverted rib cage of unknown origin rose up from the floor of bones on a stem of vertebrae. As it rose to meet Rani Grace's rear, it sort of scooped her into a sitting position, and the whole seat slid closer to the strange Uncle and stopped when it was a foot away from him.

He leaned forward, bowed his head, and folded all eight of his hands into a mandala-esque *Vanakkam*.

"Welcome *ma*, welcome!"

Now that she was closer to him Rani Grace noticed that none of the hands on the dials of his eight wristwatches were moving in the same direction.

"Do you know who I am, *chellam*?"

"No. But I have a feeling you're going to tell me," said Rani Grace, surprising herself with how cool she sounded.

"Shabash! You have solid spark I tell you! Excellent!" he said, clapping two pairs of hands together while the other four gave the thumbs up sign. Then he brought one of the hands in front of him and pointed it at his sternum.

"Myself, Boochandi," he said, with a small nod.

Rani Grace was taken back. The Boochandi was a bogeyman, a fairy-tale monster used by harassed parents, grandparents, and older siblings to threaten difficult children. *If you don't go to sleep, the Boochandi will come and take away what you love the most.* Her own mother had never told her such tall tales—it hadn't been necessary, Rani Grace had never been a difficult child—but she knew that for all the other children of Puthuyirpet, the Boochandi was the number one classic cautionary tale villain.

"Chanceless. You're a children's bedtime story," said Rani Grace.

The Boochandi chuckled heartily. The rooster turned its head towards her and made a soft clucking noise. The Boochandi stroked its neck and said to it, in a coaxing voice, "What *da* Mani, *chuch chuch chuch!* Be calm, raja, be calm." Then he turned back to his guest and continued.

"'You are very correct, my girl, you are very correct! But you yourself must know that tall tales told over countless generations eventually somehow happen to become true, no? The legend of the Boochandi has existed from so long, long ago, from the beginning of time—before all these countries, these cities... before everything was born. Arrey, before there was even electricity, ancient mothers inside caves told their *bachchas* stories about me to make them go to sleep by the light of dying bonfires. You see, my dear..." He leaned towards Rani Grace—and this time his face was fixed in its demonic aspect—"I am very real."

As he whispered these words, a lock of his hair stretched out from his head, whipped over to the nearest plant with the in-and-out needles, wrapped itself around one of the spikes, broke it off, and then—moving at lightning speed all the while—whipped back and stabbed it into Rani Grace's arm.

She yelled and dropped her spade. A proper trickle of blood flowed down to her folded kurta sleeve.

Rani Grace was mad. She rarely got mad, but this was an unprovoked surprise attack.

"Okay, so you're real, then. Why did you bring me here? What do you want?"

"Aha! Very good! Let us get to the main matter. See ma, your mother is going to die within one month. She is very sick, but neither she nor you know it yet."

"Rubbish."

"No, no, no—not *rubbish!* God Promise! She is going to pukka die," Boochandi said with childlike sincerity. "Furthermore, she cannot be cured by any doctor-shoctor Edison-medicine and all. But I, myself, can help. Of course on one small condition."

"Why should I believe anything you say?"

He snapped his fingers with three of his right hands, and pointed to Rani Grace with three of his left.

"Shabash! Balle! Correct! But my dear, how do you know I am *not* telling the truth?"

They stared at each other. The Boochandi's eyes were intense, and after a moment Rani Grace averted her gaze and looked down at his feet. She noticed that sticking out of the end of each chappal were twelve toes, all identical in size, and that at the tip of each digit there was a little opening like a mouth, from which a tiny forked snake-tongue flicked out.

When she looked back up into his eyes, she knew that what he had said about her mother was true.

"Okay, save my mother then, and in return you can have my life."

"*Th, th, th, th, th,* too easy ma, too easy!" Boochandi tut-tutted. "I like to see people having a hard time, da. Suffering is what feeds me, you know."

"Fine, so what do you want?"

"I will take your first true love."

Rani Grace stared at him. Romantic love was the farthest thing from her mind. She had never given it a thought, nor had it ever crept up on her and taken her by surprise. It just wasn't something she'd ever considered.

"Excuse me, what?"

"I said, I will take your first true love."

"Uhh… okay."

The Boochandi's eyes gleamed like two bright LED bulbs.

"Are you sure?" he said slowly. "Because when I do take them from you, you cannot say *please* and all, and beg me to give them back."

Rani Grace looked straight into those now almost blindingly bright eyes. Her own eyes hurt, but this time she refused to lower her gaze.

"I am sure," she said firmly.

Boochandi smiled and swung his legs up and down happily, like a kid on a swing. The tongues of his toes were flicking about madly.

"Super!" he said, and held out one hand for Rani Grace to shake. Reluctantly, she held out hers and shook it. Then the Boochandi cackled, withdrew his hand at super speed, and ran it through his ever-moving hair.

Rani Grace woke up in her own bed to the sound of pouring rain. She stared at the tear off calendar on the wall. The date on it was the next day.

Ten Years Later

Rani Grace did think about her meeting with the Boochandi now and then, but with every passing year it started to seem more like just a weird dream—despite the faint scar of a puncture wound on her right arm.

Her mother was alive and well, but the mantle of gravedigger had passed to Rani Grace a good five years ago.

It was mid-October, just after the seasonal heavy rains when everything in Puthuyirpet was a lush green. Rani Grace was doing her rounds of the hill, pushing a manual lawnmower, when she noticed someone sitting on the granite stone bench under the jamun tree.

It was a young woman. She waved to Rani Grace, who waved back, wondering who it was. She knew most of the regular visitors who came by and this young woman was not one of them. In fact she was sure she had never seen her before. The stranger had begun to walk briskly towards her.

"Hi," she said when she was up close.

"Hello," said Rani Grace.

"I'm Sumathi."

"Rani Grace."

Sumathi seemed around the same age as Rani Grace, give or take a few years. She had shoulder length hair that looked like it hadn't seen a comb in a week. She wore a two-sizes-too-large half-sleeved shirt with various sizes and types of screws block printed on it. Clipped inside her shirt pocket she had one Rotoring pen, Gauge 0.2, and one Hero fountain pen. Alongside them were two perfectly sharpened Nataraj pencils and a small custom-made 6-inch wooden pocket scale.

"You're the gravedigger," she said.

"Yes."

"I've just been posted to the power plant."

"Okay."

Sumathi smiled warmly. Rani Grace, not being very good at chit-chat, furiously tried to think of something else to say.

"What do you do? I mean at the power plant?"

"I'm a boiler technician."

"I see."

"This place is beautiful."

They both stood for a couple of minutes taking in the expanse of the graveyard.

"Okay, nice to meet you," said Sumathi. She turned around and went back to the granite bench. Rani Grace went back to cutting the grass. She was at it for an hour. Every now and then she would look over in the direction of the jamun tree. Sumathi was still there, reading a book while she ate something out of a steel dabba. Just as Rani Grace was pushing her lawnmower up the hill she turned back one final time to see Sumathi leaving.

Two days later, as Rani Grace and her mother were watering the plants that some of the families had planted around their relatives' graves, she saw Sumathi again, sitting in the same place on the granite bench eating from her metal dabba. Rani Grace noticed how her hair was in the same chaotic state, and though she was wearing a different shirt, she had the same array of writing tools carefully arranged in her pocket.

Sumathi waved to her, and she waved back.

Over the next few weeks, Rani Grace noted that Sumathi was the most regular amongst the regulars who visited the graveyard. It was interesting, since she was pretty sure Sumathi didn't have any loved ones buried here. Maybe she just likes cemeteries, thought Rani Grace. There were visitors like that sometimes—local history enthusiasts, or people who simply came to admire the ancient headstones.

A month later, around five in the evening, Rani Grace was digging a grave for the next day's burial. She had gone down three feet so far. "Yen Inniya Ponn Nilavae" was playing on her Walkman. Something made her look up, and she saw Sumathi standing near the edge of the pit. She took off her headphones and stuck her spade upright in the mud.

"Hello," Sumathi greeted her.

"Hello."

"If you don't mind would it be okay for me to stand around? I promise I won't be in your way."

"It's all right by me."

Rani Grace continued to dig. She kept her headphones out, but neither of the girls spoke to each other; in fact, after a while, Sumathi pulled out a manual and was studying intricate machine specs. When half an hour had passed, Rani Grace stopped digging and leaned against her spade at the bottom of the pit. She was going through something in her head that she had never had to process before.

She was feeling comfortable and completely herself in the presence of another person who was not her mother. In fact it felt… good.

The last few bits of twilight hung on in the sky waiting to be inked out by the onset of night.

"Chikki?" Sumathi called down to Rani Grace. She was kneeling at the edge of the pit looking down. Rani Grace put on her Eveready emergency lamp, her essential tool for working at night.

"What did you say?"

"Do you want chikki and some coffee? I have enough in my flask for both of us."

Rani Grace nodded. Sumathi threw down half a packet of Rajaram's chikki, which Rani Grace deftly caught. Next she lowered down a small-size, pista green Eagle thermos.

Rani Grace took it and looked up at her. She thought for a second and said,

"Hey Sumathi, do you want to come down?"

"Sure! But is that okay? I don't want be disrespectful."

"It's just a hole in the ground, today," said Rani Grace after a beat.

"How do you get back out?"

"See this rope?" Rani Grace showed her a thick rope with knots tied at intervals. It was anchored to a thick iron stake on the other side of the pit opposite to where Sumathi knelt.

"Ah! Now it makes sense. Okay, side please, I'm coming." Sumathi clumsily dropped down.

At first the two of them just stood silently side-by-side, Sumathi looking at the walls of the pit, noticing the three different layers in the wall of soil.

"Rani Grace, this is… this is amazing! These walls are perfect…" She tapped the sides.

Rani Grace did not know what to say in reply. No one had ever commented on her work before; it was just something she did. It had become second nature to her, like breathing. She had never really shared the real time workings of her skill or the nature of her work with anyone. This was all so new, and awkward and so… so… right.

"And you did it just like that!" Sumathi snapped her fingers. "I mean, don't misunderstand me, it's hard bloody work but you just did it like that… aaraam se, no tension! You clearly have a method. I was watching you, you just had it all figured… Every time you dug your spade into the ground, no hesitation!"

"Thanks. I've been doing this for a long time."

The two women looked at each other in the glare of the emergency light. Rani Grace felt something huge shift in her otherwise ordered world. She had shared something of herself with another human being. Even though they had hardly spoken, standing shoulder to shoulder in that empty grave under a star-strewn sky, Rani Grace unexpectedly felt very connected to another living soul, to another person.

A new routine added itself to Rani Grace's life. Sumathi would come to the graveyard thrice a week at 5 p.m. and hang out till around 9 p.m. They would each do their own work: Rani Grace would alternate between grave maintenance, keeping the grass trimmed, and digging new graves, while Sumathi would study her machine manuals. They would take coffee-chikki breaks, or coffee-and-keema-samosas breaks. Sometimes Sumathi would bring early dinner in her dabba for two. Books were exchanged, and mix cassette tapes. They would talk sometimes, but not too much.

Sumathi taught Rani Grace to play rummy. This game was reserved for Fridays only. Usually they would play at Rani Grace's house. Once in a while they would let her mother join the game—reluctantly, because she would invariably beat them.

Sumathi also began to call Rani Grace RG, which she realised she really, really liked.

Rani Grace had told Sumathi about how beautiful the full moon looked when framed by the rectangle of a grave pit. Sumathi wanted to see for herself. A simple plan was made for a week later. Sumathi would bring dinner—ghee rice and chicken kurma—and Rani Grace would bring the after-dinner coffee.

On the appointed night Rani Grace worked like a maestro. She started at sunset. She measured off precise coordinates with her trusted metal tape measure. She made her outline with white kollam maavu and the help of cotton twine. She anchored her rope, and then began the actual digging—her arms moving with the rhythm of an Olympic rower, she excavated spadeful after spadeful of soil, carving a perfect space inside the ground. By the time Sumathi arrived at 7:30, the pit was done.

Rani Grace was waiting for her by the granite bench.

"Hello, RG."

"Hi."

"Beautiful night," said Sumathi casually. She lowered her small cloth bag down to Rani Grace, and then, less clumsily than last time, jumped to a standing position inside the pit.

"Wow! This one's much wider that the last one, RG."

Rani Grace suddenly got awkward.

"Yeah, it... has to be. For two people to lie down and look at the moon, I mean," she said quietly.

"Of course! My brain is being slow today. Needs nourishment!"

They both climbed back out for dinner and headed to the granite bench. Sumathi pulled two steel dabbas from her cloth bag and two metal spoons. They ate dinner mostly in silence, listening to the sounds of the insects.

As they walked back to the pit, a soft boom of thunder sounded from far away.

"What, is it going to rain? The sky seems so clear!" said Sumathi.

"No chance, it must be somewhere far off, past the outskirts of town," replied Rani Grace.

Rani Grace was feeling many things she had not felt before. As she lowered herself into the ground, she gave herself a quick, silent pep talk to keep it together. She was being silly. Sumathi followed after her. They both sat by side, the emergency lamp at the end of the wall opposite to their feet.

Sumathi poured out coffee in the thermos lid for Rani Grace; she herself would drink straight from the thermos. She took a big sip and looked up. The moon was now directly over them and it looked stunning. Sumathi stood the Thermos in the slightly damp earth to her right. Then she stretched herself out, bending her right arm as a pillow under her head, and looked at the sky. A few seconds later Rani Grace lay down as well. There was about a foot of earth between them, like a rotated hyphen.

The two women stared up at the moon, which seemed to glow brighter. The more they stared, they felt as if it was growing bigger, too.

"RG, this is..." Sumathi didn't complete her sentence. She didn't have to. "Thank you," she whispered. Her hand found its way to Rani Grace's and held it tightly.

All the churning of emotions that Rani Grace had felt earlier all subsided. Now there was just a pure, quiet joy, a strong feeling she had never experienced before. Her heart was totally full. She took her eyes away from the moon and looked at Sumathi, who had also turned to look at her. Sumathi smiled...

And then, without any warning, ropes of thorny vines erupted from the earth beneath her. One vine stifled a scream that was going to come from Sumathi's mouth while another coiled around her waist and bound her hands to her back, piercing her skin with its thorns and drawing blood. Yet another vine wound itself around her feet. Sumathi's eyes were wide in terror and silently screaming at Rani Grace, who had become as still as a stone statue, helpless to do anything for the person she now knew she deeply loved.

The vines pulled Sumathi back into the ground from where they came. In seconds it was over, she was gone. Rani Grace was alone in the pit she had so masterfully dug.

She unfroze. Crying big silent tears, she dug at the earth manically with her bare hands, trying to find some piece of those wretched vines. But there was nothing, neither leaf nor tendril. Nothing remained to show that they had been there at all.

Rani Grace stopped her mad digging. She collected herself, stilled her heaving sobs, and wiped her eyes. She grabbed the rope and climbed quickly out of the pit. Her spade lay to the side. She hefted it onto her right shoulder and ran to the jamun tree. The moon had been blotted out by clouds as dense as black factory smoke. Clap after clap of thunder sounded, like evil, mocking applause. Rain began to fall hard and fast. Each drop was needle-sharp and stung Rani Grace as she ran.

When she was near the jamun tree, she expected the ground to swallow her as it had those ten years ago. But nothing happened. She stamped the ground near the tree, screaming like a wild animal. Nothing happened. She attacked the tree with her spade. Nothing. She began to dig desperately at the roots of the jamun tree.

The sky now churned with clouds and the thunder kept up its heartless clapping.

Rani Grace knew the digging was useless. She stopped, went up to the tree, and screamed.

"Come on! Let me come to you. I know you're watching! Are you enjoying yourself? Just this much is enough for you? Come on Boochandi, I thought you were a bigger player than this! Look at me! I am ready to fight! You haven't destroyed me! Don't you want to try again? Finish me off for good? How about another deal, Uncle? You said you like watching people suffer, but look at me! I'm still standing! You just took someone from me, and that's it? So easy! You're a fraud, Boochandi! A maha fraud! This is just too easy!"

This time the ground gave way beneath her feet and she was back where she had been at age sixteen, standing in the cave of bones. Everything in the cavern was the same as it was the first time around. The Boochandi had not aged a day, and neither had Mani the rooster. The Boochandi was lying on the curve of its ample back like an Uncle enjoying a hammock on a timeshare holiday. This time his safari suit was sunflower yellow velvet. He turned his head slowly to Rani Grace.

"What ma! Apapapapapaa! What screaming and shouting! Eh? Can't take any rest! I try to close my eyes but no! I can hear your *keech keech keech* shouting! Giving me severe migraine, I tell you!"

"Where is she?"

"Where is who, ma? Ah, your buddy!" The Boochandi chuckled heartily and waved a single left hand. To the left side of rooster, the cave walls parted like a slash. A thick flood of thorny vines cascaded out like a mini waterfall. They held aloft Sumathi, whose face alone was visible, the rest of her entombed in a cocoon of vines. Her eyes were open, but had a dead, unblinking stare.

"Sumathi!" screamed Rani Grace and started to run to her. Vines broke through the floor of bones on either side of her and coiled rapidly around her feet and legs, anchoring her back to the place she had stood before.

Boochandi shook his head.

"Useless! Just what are you trying to do my dear? Hmmm? You think you can save your Sumathi, ah??" Boochandi gave a hearty laugh and slapped both thighs once with each of his hands.

"Haiyo! I tell you ma, you are most excellent entertainment! Arrey, how can you save her? You cannot! She is mine now. She belongs to Boochandi. You only gave me the promise, no? Correct?"

"Correct. I gave you my word."

"Then? Now why all this tamasha eh?"

Rani Grace inhaled deeply.

"Boochandi, don't you know sometimes promises are made to be broken?"

The rooster turned its head towards Rani Grace and stared at her for just a moment with its black glass marble eyes. Rani Grace felt the red glow of its pulsating heart glow a shade stronger.

"Ahhahahaha! You think you are in a motion picture or what? Giving dialog it seems! Rubbish!"

"Where is the thrill for you? I made a promise. And that's it, you come after ten years and take away the person I fell in love with. Tell me truly, don't you think it's too simple? After all, that's nothing for someone like you and your powers."

The Boochandi flinched noticeably at that last line. Rani Grace knew she had him figured him out now—he was proud and vain and liked big grand gestures. He couldn't handle the idea that a mortal woman could put dents in his grand design, his guaranteed sure-shot victory.

"Of course, if this is enough for you, then fine, send me home. I will understand of you don't want a real challenge…"

"Challenge ah? Challenge? You dare to challenge me?" yelled the Boochandi, now standing on top of the rooster's back and shaking with rage. "You…!" he brought up his first left hand and began to make an action like he was squeezing the air between his thumb and forefinger.

The rooster vibrated like a struck soundless bell. The red of its heart got deeper in hue.

Rani Grace's legs folded like up like a chair. She doubled over, with her hands across her chest. She was choking—the Boochandi was squeezing the air out of her lungs. Her eyes felt like they were popping out of her head. They were watering madly.

Then, suddenly, the Boochandi released his grip. Rani Grace fell on the bones below, gasping like a fish out of water as air filled inside her again.

When she had regained a grip on herself, she staggered unsteadily to a standing position. Her eyes were bloodshot and still streaming with water. Her chest cavity hurt, her throat felt like someone had taken a razor to it, and she was bleeding from the forehead—she'd cut herself on a sharp shard of bone while falling. Her breathing was not yet back to normal, but at least she wasn't heaving anymore. She looked straight into the face of the bogeyman and gave him a sideways grin.

The Boochandi stared at her. This was not what he had planned. She could see him cursing himself for letting her in in the first place. He had thought it might be fun to play with her a bit before sending her back to the surface world, to taunt and torment her by showing her the other girl, to enjoy watching her pain and grief. But now she was getting the upper hand and openly challenging him. And it was too late to simply finish her off. The situation had become a prestige issue for the Boochandi.

"So is that all you have Boochandi? You're just going to use your powers to kill me? What a showman you are, truly great!" wheezed Rani Grace. She gave a slow clap.

"Pah! Why should I dirty my hands with your pathetic death? You are a waste! You give a promise and then make demands to take it back and then I am the one in the wrong?' The Boochandi was starting to sound cocky again.

"You never played fair in the first place, Mr. Boochandi. You asked for something you know nobody can give you."

"Ah but then you were so ready. You didn't even pause to blink. You agreed at once—it was nothing for you!"

"It's not nothing for me anymore. I'm ready to fight you for the right to take back my words. But not like this. I have no tricks, no powers… no magic. Come down and fight me person to pers— to whatever you are."

The Boochandi rolled his eyes and cracked all the knuckles on all his left hands with his right ones.

"Ma, that is not how it works."

"Why are you frightened?" Rani Grace chuckled wheezily.

The rooster turned towards her again. Its jet-black beak was slightly parted, as if it were trying to smile. Its whole chest glowed red now, like a Chinese paper lantern. Rani Grace knew what she had to do.

"Don't simply provoke me, you wretched woman!" The Boochandi was getting incensed.

"Why, what will you do?" taunted Rani Grace "You won't kill me, you won't fight me... You have no more guts than that chicken you're sitting on. *Payantha kozhi!* What a joke!"

The Boochandi's face contorted into a visage of pure evil rage. He raised his eight hands up, giant thorns appeared in each of them, and with a battle cry he leapt off the rooster's back towards Rani Grace.

Collecting all the strength she had left inside her, she raised her spade in both hands. With a yell she thrust the weapon hard into the giant rooster's chest, shattering its giant breast bone and impaling it through the heart.

In mid-air the Boochandi wailed and disintegrated into a shower of small stones. The rooster let out a plaintive squawk and then fell heavily on its side. Blood so dark it was almost black flowed like oil from the wound and began to spread.

Rani Grace collapsed to the floor. The bones began to melt away and the plants began to wilt; the cocoon of vines holding Sumathi withered, and she fell gently to the floor. Rani Grace crawled to her and picked her up. Sumathi was still in a deep sleep. She held her to her chest and shut her eyes. Around her, everything continued to melt away and disappear.

Sumathi's eyes abruptly opened. She felt heavy-headed and slightly disoriented. She looked up. The full moon looked back at her, framed by a rectangle made of freshly dug earth. She sat up and found a strangely disheveled Rani Grace leaning her head against her upright spade, looking at her.

"Hey, have I been sleeping for a long time?"

"No, just a few minutes."

They looked at each other for a moment and then, as if on cue, both turned their heads skywards.

"The full moon really does look amazing from inside here, RG."

"I'm telling you: there's a lot more you can discover inside a freshly dug grave," said Rani Grace, reaching once more for Sumathi's hand.

EXTRADIMENSIONAL THANKS TO THE FOLLOWING PEOPLE, WITHOUT WHOSE SUPPORT THE BANDIGOAT COULD NOT HAVE MATERIALISED

Vinayak Hegde
Hari Krishna Vetharenian
Zack Fissel
Ruth Ann Orlansky
Tejas
Devdas Bhagat
Alexandra Carrillo
Kaye Lofgreen
Rachel Yelding
Smit
Finbarr Farragher
August Quinn
Noarvara
Eric Beauchamp
Rev. Slick Sellers
Steve Pattee
Brain Vs Book
Rosco Lance
Niveditha Sundar
Kevin Halstead
Mark Alexander
Andrew Roach
A
Tim
Brian D. Smith
Enteroctopus dofleini
Rimi B. Chatterjee
Goldwin Fonseca
Binti Mfalme Bhabya Tewari
Florentina
Skye Sisk
Kalloway
Orijit Sen / People Tree Studio
Saurabh Yadav
Eric B.
Nidhi Salian
H Conley
Serena Lukas Bhandar
Terri the Goblin
Prathamesh Kapse
Joyce Chng

Simrita
M
Charudatta Bandgar
Joshua Cooper
Malusdraco
Paromita Vohra
Rashmi
Kruti
Marie Khan
Trip Space-Parasite
Aditi Goyal
Safdar
Podigai Nemo
Abhijeet Sathe
Axel Kallesøe
Shweta Swaminathan
Shaun Williams
Seth Davis
Atthis Arts
Varun
Rohini Malur
Hew
Preethi & Sharanya Vemu
Esther Larisa
Ankur Tibrewala
Mara Thacker
Tom Speaker
After Harville
Chhavi Sachdev
Chatterine Nongag
Jeffrey Hill
Emma Katherine
Colleen Feeney
Virender Murkblob
Isha Karki
Amanda W
Jonathan Soriano
Nimesha Tadepalle
Wickie
Reperzell

Bogi Takács
Andrea Tatjana
Minal Hajratwala
Sujith Venkatesh
Aravind
Wayne Mook
Robert ORourke
Alex D
Saurabh Kumar
Viktor
Susan Parrott
Adrienne Shaffer
Serpent_moon
Melissa
Brandy Pastore
Divya Manian
Alysia Cooper
Konsectatrix
Alex Zucker
Daisy Patton
This Ryan
Lotta Fjelkegård
Nira
Katie Molloy
Steph Kelley
Joyce Pusel
Kaushik
Roxy Fanshier-Haggard
Ollie Feldman
Kelly Hoolihan
Elias Jacob Albarracin
Vivek Nityananda
Ernfrid
Marissa Armstrong
Larry Jorash, Jr.
Kelsey Griffiths
Soniya Kulkarni
Wendy Mann
Yasir Husain
Ranjit Bhatnagar
Bill Halliar II

ABOUT THE CONTIBUTORS

Rakesh Khanna was born in Berkeley, California and now lives in Chennai. He co-founded Blaft Publications in 2008. He is the co author of *Ghosts, Monsters, and Demons of India*, the editor of *The Blaft Anthology of Tamil Pulp Fiction* and *The Blaft Anthology of Gujarati Pulp Fiction*, and co-editor of *The Blaft Book of Anti-Caste SF.*

Srividya Tadepalli is a writer and poet based in Chennai. She won the Deodar Prize in 2023 for "Funeral for a Demon". She is the biological mother of two cats.

Kuzhali Manickavel's short story collections, chapbooks and ezines are available from Blaft Publications. Her work has also appeared in *Granta*, *Strange Horizons*, *The White Review*, *AGNI*, *Subtropics*, *Michigan Quarterly Review* and *DIAGRAM*. More information can be found at www.kuzhalimanickavel.com.

Lungmying Lepcha is an aspiring poet and creative director from Sikkim. A keen listener, she has always taken an interest in her roots, especially the folktales of her ancestors and her culture. Her story in this collection was born from listening to those tales while looking out over squash plants growing by the electricity pole. You can keep her track of her ideas on Instagram: @aamiklom.

M. L. Krishnan originally hails from the coastal shores of Tamil Nadu. She has been awarded Fellowships and Residencies from Tin House, MacDowell, the Carnegie Corporation, Millay Arts, and the Clarion West Writers Workshop. Her stories and essays have appeared or are forthcoming in *Fantasy*, *Strange Horizons*, *Black Warrior Review* and elsewhere. Her work has been anthologised in *The Year's Best Dark Fantasy & Horror*, *Brave New Weird*, *Afterlives: The Year's Best Death Fiction*, *Wigleaf Top 50*, *Best Microfiction*, *Best Small Fictions* and more. You can find her at mlkrishnan.com.

Miriam Kumaradoss-Hohauser's writing has appeared in *Apogee Journal* (where they also served as Fiction Editor), *CrimeReads*, *Literary Hub*, *Cosmonauts Avenue*, and elsewhere. They grew up in South India and now live in New York City, where they are working on their first novel.

Jugal Mody is a storyteller, artist and new media producer. His first novel *Toke* (HarperCollins India) was about stoners saving the world from zombies. In his second novel, *Turds of Gold* (HarperCollins India), a superhero with laxative superpowers fights a gastric pandemic and blind faith. Between the two novels, Jugal wrote Indian actor and star Alia Bhatt's official mobile game, *Alia Bhatt: Star Life*, an adventure set in the Hindi film industry. He also was a consulting editor with the award-winning feminist magazine *The Ladies Finger* and has collaborated on projects with comedian Aditi Mittal and online platform Brainded India.

Rashmi Ruth Devadasan is a co-founder of Blaft Publications who has also worked in feature films and Indian English theatre. She is the author of *Kumari Loves a Monster*, a picture book created with the artist Shyam, and several short stories about zombies. She is a fan of fungi, moss, lichen, cephalopods, and jellyfish. Rashmi also draws gentle sample collector robots on a cacti-covered asteroid called Succulentious. These can be found on the 'Gram under the handle @kaimaurundai.

Misha Michael, a.k.a. Madame Bandigoat, finds it extremely difficult to write bios.